P9-AOK-258

DISCARDED

Rebecca Rosenblum, Daniel Griffin & Alice Petersen

COMING ATTRACTIONS
08

We acknowledge the support of the Canada Council for the Arts, the Ontario Arts Council, the Government of Ontario through the Ontario Media Development Corporation and the Government of Canada through the Book Publishing Industry Development Program for our publishing activities.

An earlier version of "The House on Elsbeth" by Rebecca Rosenblum first appeared in *The New Quarterly*. "Mercedes Buyer's Guide" by Daniel Griffin was first published in *The Dalhousie Review* and *Journey Prize Stories 16*. "Promise" by Daniel Griffin originally appeared in *The Wisconsin Review*. "'X'" by Daniel Griffin was first published in *Prairie Fire*. "After Summer" by Alice Petersen first appeared in *Geist* and *Journey Prize Stories 19*. "Salsa Madre" by Alice Petersen was originally published in *Geist*.

ISBN 978 0 7780 1321 1 (hardcover)
ISBN 978 0 7780 1322 8 (softcover)

Cover art from a bestiary published in 1500
Book design by Michael Macklem

Printed in Canada

PUBLISHED IN CANADA BY OBERON PRESS

Canada Council for the Arts   Conseil des Arts du Canada   ONTARIO ARTS COUNCIL CONSEIL DES ARTS DE L'ONTARIO

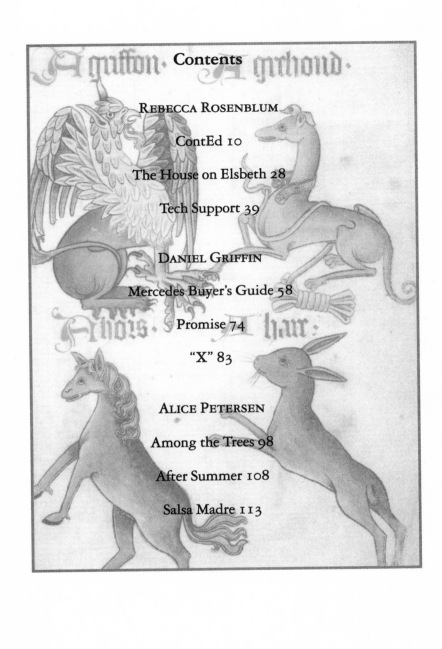

Contents

REBECCA ROSENBLUM

ContEd 10

The House on Elsbeth 28

Tech Support 39

DANIEL GRIFFIN

Mercedes Buyer's Guide 58

Promise 74

"X" 83

ALICE PETERSEN

Among the Trees 98

After Summer 108

Salsa Madre 113

INTRODUCTION

This collection is a very strong showing. These three vibrant writers, Rebecca Rosenblum, Daniel Griffin and Alice Petersen, are not caught in easy binaries; they can cover rural lanes or urban terrains, they can do kitchen sink or blood on the palace walls, they can cover the waterfront.

Rebecca Rosenblum has been creating a buzz in publishing circles with offbeat, innovative pieces appearing in many good magazines and in the Journey Prize anthology; a first collection will be published very soon. Rosenblum's characters are habitués of an ex-urban strip-mall world similar to *Repo Man*'s Edge City: techno-geek workers grapple with office politics and court and spark as skaters zip past the windows. And she places an Edmonton Oilers toque in one story, which makes me especially happy.

Daniel Griffin, who lives in Victoria, has also been included in the Journey Prize anthology, is publishing in Canadian and American magazines, and has been shortlisted for the CBC Literary Awards. His evocative stories detail the X factors and complexities of shifting domestic roles for males and females; Griffin writes ably of brothers and fathers, mothers and sons, weapons and drugs, and guilt and relief in a new century.

Alice Petersen writes compelling, painterly tales of New Zealand and North America; her prose is assured and sophisticated, boasting wedding-cake layers of narrative. Petersen has been published in many journals, including *The Fiddlehead*, *Geist*, and *Takahe*, a New Zealand magazine. She has also been included in the Journey Prize anthology and nominated for a National Magazine Award. She is a joy to discover.

MARK ANTHONY JARMAN

Contributions for Coming Attractions 09, *published or unpublished, should be sent to Oberon Press, 205–145 Spruce Street, Ottawa, Ontario* KI R 6PI *before 31 March, 2009. All manuscripts should enclose a stamped self-addressed envelope.*

REBECCA ROSENBLUM

ContEd

Eva's Place is busiest in the evenings—lots of fried cheese and ass-grabbing near midnight. We're supposed to close at one, but drunk people are hard to scatter. It's good tips, and I got used to sloppy pub scenes when I hung around with Riley, my ex. I just don't like getting home so late there's not enough time for sleeping, cooking, errands, let alone reading. *Tax Answers* is boring, but I understand if I concentrate. When I'm tired, I wind up staring at the same page until I fall asleep. The book cost $60.

By the time I get to the campus I have ten minutes to find the classroom. I meant to stop and eat. I meant to look calm and smart, not confused and late. The Continuing Education people sent me a map that I can't follow, a little notebook, a ruler, a pen, all printed with *ContEd*. As I walk, I keep thinking ContEd isn't a real word. My feet hurt and the interconnected buildings make no sense; when I look out a window I'm across the street from where I started.

I only notice the room number because a man with red-blond hair is closing the door. "Oh," I call so he'll wait. I feel like if I get there before the door closes, I'm not really late. I try to catch his eye and smile, but he's not paying attention. He's got loafers on, too, shinier than mine.

There's about 30 desks and orange plastic chairs, mainly taken. I don't look at anyone, just push toward the only empty seat—in the far corner, of course—*sorryexcusemesorry*. The man in loafers stands at the front, tossing a piece of chalk. He's got serious glasses, serious loafers, but a soft pink mouth, and a shaving cut on his chin.

"Welcome, everyone, to Introductory Tax Preparation, an opportunity to learn about your own taxes as well as move toward becoming a professional tax preparer, a fascinating career. I'm Barton Denby, and I'm a tax guy, and...well, it's a fascinating career. Now, you can all introduce yourselves, and then we'll do a quick quiz to see what skill level we're working with. Ummm, could you start...." He kind of just waves at the left side of the room, but a cute Asian girl with tiny pigtails answers.

"Hi, Mr. Denby. I'm Ling. Last year we got audited and my husband sent me here to make sure that *never* happens again." She grins and bounces her crossed leg.

"Just Barton, please. This is ContEd, we're all adults." He says ContEd like it's a real word.

"I'm Jeff, and I'm a bank teller. Um, yeah." Jeff seems nervous for someone who talks for work, shuffling his laceups under his desk. Then again, I'm nervous too. It didn't occur to me that I'd have talk in front of everyone. I thought I could just listen, do the homework, see how it goes.

"I'm Marina. I've been a stay-at-home mom for 23 years, and now I'd like to get into the exciting world of business." Marina keeps looking at her long navy dress, touching it. It must be the best thing she owns.

"I'm Stevey. My EI says I gotta re-train for something. I used to do carpet-cleaner rentals." Stevey's shirt has a nametag that says *Lou*, and he's wearing dirty white sneakers with the laces undone.

It's my turn. In high-school math, I usually got sixties, but that was without ever trying. Riley said I was too smart for homework, or even to go to class. When I paid attention, it seemed easy. "I'm Isobel. I used to be good at math."

The quiz is hard. I only brought my ContEd pen, so I have to cross out mistakes, which looks awful. We mark ourselves since the quiz doesn't count, but I still feel stupid.

I get 74%, and then someone asks if class is over. The teacher looks surprised, but he says yes. It's nearly nine when I get on the streetcar and open the box of leftovers Eva gave me. Beautiful highlight-hair high-school girls glare across the aisle when I get rice on the floor. This whole night felt like high school. But that was a long time ago, and back then I didn't even really care.

At home, I take off my shoes before I turn on the lights. Blood rushes into my feet, tingling and pinging like fireworks. It feels so good I almost can't stand it. I lie on the couch and try to read the textbook, but I'm too sleepy. When the phone rings, I don't answer. When it stops, I set the alarm clock and turn off the light.

On Tuesday I try reading on my break. When it's raining, the only break spot is the back of the kitchen, where everyone can see you. I wish I could sit in the alley.

"That literature, Iz?" Eva asks.

Mara, another dinner waitress, laughs before I can answer, which is just as well, since I haven't got one. "I always thought you were deep, Iz. That's how quiet ones are."

"It's a tax textbook."

"Oh," Mara says. She's about eight months pregnant, her belly poking out under her apron. "Why?"

I shrug. Eva slams a brick of ground beef onto the counter. "Yeah, Iz, you checking up on our honesty?" She and Mara start plucking wads of meat from the brick and weighing them on the little scale. Three ounces, roll twice in your hands, put it between two sheets of waxed paper and press it flat: tomorrow's hamburgers.

"Just seemed like...something to do."

"Ah, you need a boyfriend, you got too much free time, Iz."

I do need a boyfriend, but I don't even have time to get the reading done before Thursday. I wear my work blouse and a blue skirt. I'm cold and the skirt looks stupid with Docs, but I don't have gravy on me and my feet don't hurt. Much.

Barton's got a blue tie this week, but still no jacket. I wonder if he was cold on the way over, too. He has neat fingernails, no wedding ring, loafers again. I wonder if his feet hurt—shiny shoes are usually stiff, too.

"One of the most satisfying things about tax preparation is all that you can learn about human nature. You become like a confessor. People tell you *any*thing, like a doctor." I underline *confessor* in my notes. I can't imagine anyone confessing anything to me, or me being able to help. I'd like to, though.

"Questions about the intro chapter?" Stevey didn't know we were supposed to read anything. Ling couldn't find the textbook at the bookstore. Lachlan doesn't know what a "common-law partnership" is.

"Well, um, that refers to individuals in a conjugal relationship, two adults who share residence and financial resources to some degree, um, maybe kids."

"So living in sin. A man and a woman not married."

I think Barton rolls his eyes, but I'm sitting in the back again, so I can't be sure. I wasn't late this time, but everyone else sat in the same seats as before, so I did, too. "Yeah, basically. But—" Barton fists up his fingers around the chalk "— it could be a man and a woman, or two men or two women—"

"Whoa, now, Revenue Canada will count two men as a *marr*iage?" Lachlan's voice is very loud. Marina goes and shuts the door to the hallway.

"Not a, not a marriage. Partnership. And it's not Revenue Canada anymore, it's actually called Canada Revenue Agency.... Anyotherquestions?"

Lachlan raises his hand, but Barton is staring at the ceiling. For a minute we all just sit quietly. Then Marina calls, "Weren't we supposed to have a quiz?"

"Yes, right now."

I remembered to bring a pencil this week, which is good since I need to erase half of what I write down. Barton reads something called *The 48 Laws of Power* while we write. I guess teachers trust adult classes.

After the quiz, Barton shows a T4 and talks about how "non-exceptions" would fill it out. There are lots of questions, even though it's just what everybody does every April. People seem to ask stuff almost at random in this class, about pets and separate school boards and home repairs. Lachlan brings up common-law partnerships again, asking if couples can file together if they aren't married.

"Um, is that in the text? It shouldn't be in the text. You *can't* file jointly in Canada. That's an American thing." Barton plays with his chalk, making little white marks on his blue cuff and then rubbing them out.

"Well, in the States, then?"

Barton drops the chalk and he can't seem to grab it from the floor. "I only do Canadian stuff," he says from upside down. "This class doesn't cover US law."

Ling starts talking about an American TV show where accountants are also detectives. Barton finally stands up with the chalk and notices it's 9.07 and says, "We'll pick this up next week." His face is red, maybe from being upside down.

As I walk past him toward the door, he looks up and asks, "How was the quiz?" He's shoving notes into his bag. "Easy? Hard?"

I start stacking the leftover handouts and papercut the inside of my thumb. I want to say it was easy, but he's going to mark my paper. "Hard, because I didn't finish the reading." I hand him the pages. There's blood on the edges, but he doesn't notice.

"Was there too much?" He zips his bag closed, open, closed.

"I just didn't get time. I'll catch up."

"It's not supposed to be stressful. I used to make myself crazy over tough classes. I wouldn't want to do that to you guys."

"I just want to do well."

"Just speak up when you don't understand." He holds the door open and we walk out into the hallway. "No shame in asking questions."

He thinks I'm in the same category as Stevey, who thinks

cats are dependants. I duck into the ladies' room so I won't have to take the elevator with him.

Eva's probably only about 35, and Mara's younger than that, but they act like old mamas, like pretty clothes and parties are a waste of time and so is trying to be nice when you don't mean it. A few things are the same in Toronto as they were in Montreal, and one is ladies like Eva and Mara, who seem to have been born married.

They never use their husbands' names, just *he him his*. When they call *him* on the telephone they don't say hello, just start talking. Sometimes Eva and Mara come in to work with dirty hair because their husbands take really long showers. Sometimes they look in their purses and their cigarettes aren't there because the husbands are smoking them. If it weren't for their husbands, Eva and Mara would never screw anything up, ever. They are always tired but beautiful, and they made their own wedding dresses and talk to their mothers every day. They can snatch their purses back from muggers and carry three plates on each arm.

They feel bad for me, because I don't have any family in the city, because I'm a bad waitress, because I'm single. I never told them much about Riley, but somehow they figured out that there was a man in Montreal and now I'm alone. They want to help, but don't really have too many ideas.

"That guy on table fourteen was cute."

"With the little baby?"

"Yeah, but no lady friend. Single dad? You should ask him out."

Mara comes in clutching three empty coffeepots above her bump. "Yeah! Who?"

"Table fourteen."

"Oh, yeah, very cute. You can write your phone number on the back of his bill."

"I don't think that's a good idea."

15

"No, really, I saw it in a movie once. Or in a song, maybe, a country song?"

I couldn't do it, but they still look for men for me. It's what they've come up with.

I have Mondays off, which Riley knows about, so the phone rings and rings. I used to answer sometimes, but we never had anything to say. I imagine telling him about Eva's, taxes, school. The only part I can imagine him understanding is how much my feet hurt—he works construction, when he's working. After a long shift, I feel it even in my ankles, even in my knees. Even the papercut stings more when I'm tired.

The ringing distracts me from studying, so I go out for lunch. The Vietnamese sandwich place because it's cheap and I won't need to be waited on. I don't know what the meat on the bun is, but I get all the reading done. Then I make a summary, like the ContEd study guide said. When I get tired, I underline the headings in red. It looks smart.

A relationship of a conjugal nature, a sharing of resources. In high school, Riley gave me my own keys to his truck so I could drive myself to work after school if he ditched or got too trashed in the woods. His truck, but mine to use. By the time we'd started living together, he'd totalled the truck so bad he couldn't get it repaired, but then we split the rent. Is an apartment a resource? We lived there together a long time. Could Riley and I have been a partnership and never even known it?

Around six I go back to the counter and order another sandwich for supper. If the cashier notices that I've been there for five hours, he doesn't say. He has a hairnet, big bags under his eyes, but a nice smile, small and quiet. Is he cute? Is he smiling at me because he thinks I'm cute? How does anyone ever know? I go back to my plastic table and my books.

On Thursday, we get our quizzes back. 52%. Barton just made slashes through the wrong answers, as if he trusted me to find the right ones. I did. I know home office expenses and per diems, front to back. I'm sure I aced the quiz this week. Pretty sure.

Last two classes, I was dizzy hungry by the end, so today I have a couple of Eva's baklava, free and filling. It's hard to eat something sticky and take notes at the same time, though. At the end of class, I'm still working on my first piece.

Barton wanders toward me with his eyebrows up and interested. "What's that?"

"It's baklava." His eyebrows stay high. "It's a Greek dessert, honey and nuts and pastry. Want one?" I hold out the box. I don't think I need to tell that they're old.

"Um. Sure." He peels a pastry off the waxed paper and pops it whole into his mouth. I wouldn't have done that—I should've warned him. His eyes bug out, but no crumbs escape, no choking. I jam the box into my bag. "Have a good night, then."

He keeps chewing. His face is starting to go a bit red, but he waves as I leave.

When I left Riley, it was for good. Once I'd decided, it was easy to quit my job, buy the bus ticket, pack while he was at work, go. Everybody said Toronto had cleaner streets, cleaner men, nicer weather than Montreal. That seems true, but in a year I haven't seen much. I wonder how you meet people when you don't know anyone to introduce you. I go to work and home and work. I see Toronto when the subway car bursts into the light before Broadview.

When I first got here, I didn't see the harm in letting Riley know my new number, that I'm all right, that I don't miss him. He didn't have much to say to that, or to anything, but he still calls, calls, and says nothing. Maybe it's because he loves me, but it doesn't feel like that. Still, at least someone calls.

Mara comes in with a stack of paper towels. The staff bathroom is really only for one person, no stalls. The lock broke ages ago, though, and waitresses aren't too polite when they're rushing. I'm just pulling my skirt over my hips, so I'm not too embarrassed. I fold my work pants into my bag.

"All dressed up for class?" Mara tries to jam the towels into the dispenser. She pushes the door up partway with her shoulder, but it's dented so she can't get it fully open. A few paper towels drift to the wet floor. "How's that going?"

"It's okay. But pretty hard, and there's some weirdos."

"Well, it *is* a whole class about taxes—what'd you expect?"

I don't want to tell her I think new people, even weirdos, are better than no people. "Barton says, when you do someone's taxes, you find out people's secrets and become a student of human nature."

"Oh." Mara jolts up suddenly and the metal door bangs back against the wall. "Aha!" She shoves the towels in. "Who's Barton?"

"The teacher." I take my hair down, but there's a dent from the elastic like a reverse halo. I put it back up.

"You call your teacher by his first name?"

"Sure. We're all adults. He's not that much older than me."

Mara's eyes snap wide. "Is he cute? Does he like Greek food?"

I pick up the soggy paper and stuff it in the trash. "He liked Eva's baklava."

"You guys shared food?" Mara makes a noise like she's cheering at a football game. "So you like him? He's cute? You should ask him out."

"Um." Another waitress, Deena, comes in and squeezes between us, already hiking up her skirt. Mara rolls her eyes and goes out and I think that's the end of it. Later, though, Eva gives me a whole box of mini-baklavas. She says that desserts are slow, these are gonna go off before they sell, but sugar and nuts don't spoil. Plus she winks.

During class, Barton says his bosses sometimes hire his best students for tax season. "It's a good way to get started in the industry."

"Did you take a course like ours?" Ling asks dreamily.

"I'm actually—I trained as a lawyer, but then I...decided that my strengths lay elsewhere." He suddenly bends over and ties his shoe very carefully. Everybody's quiet. If you have to go to law school to be a real tax person, the ContEd catalogue should've said that. Barton stands up and starts talking about artistic grants.

I stay after class to give Barton the pastries. Plus, I have a list of questions for him. Mara told me men like being asked about things. So I read an article about Stephen Harper's tax plan. Actually, the article was interesting. I'd like to know the answers to my questions.

Lachlan is asking about the assignment, The Pazzi Family Tax Return. "So this Italian family has two cars and a cottage in Muskoka?"

"Yes. See, there on the handout."

"Now, but wait, though—trick assignment? Is *every*thing declared?"

"C'mon, Lachlan, work with the info. Explore the assignment—yes, Isobel?" People mainly call me Isobel when they're reading my nametag. "You had a question?"

I don't—all the stuff I memorized about Stephen Harper has disappeared. Finally, I remember something else. "What you said about tax preparers being confessors—"

"Um, I guess I was being a bit much." He turns the projector off. "Most of the time you just take the receipts and do the math." Lachlan shuffles out.

"But what if your client doesn't trust you? What if they lie?"

"Well, Isobel, I think I can spot a liar. I try to be perceptive." IS-oh-bell—he says it very anglo—the S sounds like an S, not a Z. He heads out, so I have to follow. "The most important thing is that you have to keep your hands clean. Totally. The client would totally be getting you to take the fall for them if you signed off on a false return. Some people will try— Well. Anyway. It's usually just dull."

"Okay." The elevator *bings*. We go in and stand in silence until the ground floor.

"Well, I'll see you next week, Isobel." He starts to walk away, then turns back. "If that answers your question, of course. Does it?"

"Sure. Um, wait." I pull the smushed box from my bag. "Since you liked that baklava, I brought you some more." The box looks like something from the garbage. He probably doesn't even remember about last week.

He takes it. "Well, thanks, Isobel. You're very sweet." He rolls his eyes.

"What?"

"Just, what a dumb joke, to say you were sweet for bringing me sweets."

"That's okay." We just stand there staring at the box until I say, "Well, bye," and go. I don't know where Barton is heading, but probably not in the same direction as me.

On Saturday night, a skinny guy in a soccer shirt corners me by the coffee station. "I like the way you work. You keep your head down, don't take no guff. These assholes, they'll take advantage. You got to keep your head down."

"Yeah?" I want to put grounds in the coffee machine just to do something, even though it's past ten and this late we only do instant. "Sure." I try to smile a little sexy, with just the side of my mouth. It feels funny.

"Really, though, you're too good to be in a place like this. Where you from, really?" He's got his hand on the counter, sliding along.

"Um, Montreal. But I like it here. It's okay."

He smiles and his hand jumps up, hooks the side of my

waist. Maybe it's friendly. It doesn't feel friendly.

"It's a nice place, really."

Sliding up to the bottom of my bra. "*These* kinds of assholes don't know nothing."

"What sort of asshole are you, then?" I don't smile at all, which feels a lot better.

He doesn't say anything, just marches off fast to his table and stares out the window for a while. He's sitting alone. I keep an eye on him.

I usually know better than to start a fight with a creepy guy. Fighting is a way of playing along, and you never play along with a creepy guy. When I'm settling up with a big group, I see him go marching up to Eva at the till. His steps are high-assed and angry, as if the thing happened two minutes ago instead of an hour.

I have to watch the conversation while the group in front of me tries to remember who drank what. I see the guy talking, shaking his head hard. Eva shakes her head, too. I can tell by his mouth he's raising his voice, even though I can't hear him over the music and the chatter. Eva starts to turn and he grabs her shoulder to stop her. I'm sure that's all he wants, to stop her, but you shouldn't grab someone like Eva. You shouldn't grab anyone. She shoves him back hard and he crashes into an unbussed table. He hits loud—so much noise for ten dollars worth of glasses. Eva calls one of the grillmen, Jamie, to haul him out. The guy tries to leave ahead of Jamie, but he keeps turning around to yell, so he ends up getting pulled out after all.

My group pays up and gets out fast. They give a huge tip. Probably added wrong, scared. A bunch of students.

I go apologize. "I shouldn't've.... Obviously. I'm sorry."

"What? He was a dick. And crazy, obviously. You're supposed to take that?"

"Well, yeah. But—"

"Hey! Mara said you said your teacher was cute. Are you

gonna ask him out?"

It takes me a minute to switch from the creepy guy to Barton. "I don't know."

"You should. Accountant's a good job. Shows he's serious, respectable, a hard worker. And you think he's cute?"

"I—" I think about Barton's washy orange hair, his small glasses and pink mouth. Those things aren't cute. I think about his shoulders underneath his thin shirt, thick and wide. He looks like someone you could lean against and be comfortable. Is that cute? "I don't think I've ever really asked a guy out."

Eva fiddles with her order pad. "Me neither. My husband handed me a beer at a party in Grade 10." Eva not knowing something feels so strange.

"Did you know all along you were going to end up marrying him?"

"No—well—I guess—I never thought about anything in the future except with him there, too. That's like knowing."

I actually don't think it is. I thought that way about Riley, but I didn't know how anything would be, that'd he drink like Saturday every night and always seem to be looking at the wall behind my head.

On Sunday, Jamie scalds his chest draining the deep fryer. Emergency-room, third degree burns, waitresses throwing lamb chops on the grill—a big mess. The next night, Mara goes into labour right at the coffee station, and then on Tuesday Deena quits from all the pressure and craziness. Eva begs me to work Thursday night. I feel like I can't say no. Besides, paying the tuition has made me need the money more. I guess that's ironic.

It's raining when I leave work and I don't know where my umbrella is. My blouse soaks and clings. It might be sexy with a different bra, on a different person.

I come in early and take a seat up front. There's raindrops

on my calculator, but it still turns on. Barton puts some papers on my desk, and my hair drips on them.

Barton smiles. "I—We—missed you last week. Were you sick?"

"I just had to work. What happened?"

Barton squats down next to me, arms folded on my desk. His sleeves get wet. "Just a review of GST, charitable donations, some provincial stuff. Read the dittos." He nods at the pages, and then we don't say anything for a minute. I wonder if there's a way I'm supposed to make him like me. I'm still thinking when Barton stands up and says in a talking-to-everybody voice, "Let's begin."

After class, Barton tries to get his umbrella over us both. "You live far, Isobel?"

"No, a bit west."

"I'll drive you. My car's just over.... I mean, if you want?"

I think that's what I want.

Barton sees me shivering and puts the heat on. My feet itch and throb as they warm up. I don't smell wet shoes—I hope Barton can't.

The last time I was in a car was when I took a cab from the station to my new apartment, a year ago. Someone back home told me about the building. The windows were greasy and the sink made noises but it was all right. I was lucky. When I give the directions to Barton, though, he asks me if I usually go home alone this late.

"It's fine, really." I shrug. "Where do you live?"

"West...Etobicoke."

It takes me a minute to picture the map. "That's pretty far."

"It's easier if you drive. And it's not forever."

"Rent's cheaper farther out. I'd do it if I had a car."

He carefully pulls his elbow in when he shifts gears so he doesn't brush me. "I'm saving to buy a condo."

"Wow," I say, but he's still speaking.

"So I'm in my folks' basement until real estate gets more reasonable, you know?"

"That makes sense." I wonder how old he is. Older than me, but not that much.

"They've got a basement apartment and I can help out with...stuff.... Geez, 9.30 already. Isobel, you must be tired?"

"Well, my feet hurt. Sometimes taking off my shoes is the sexiest part of my day." I must be tired—that's a thing I think in my head, not say out loud. I can feel the blush in my neck, At least it's too dark for him to see. "Not today, though." That's worse.

"That's, um, ah, interesting. Very interesting."

I see my awning. "This is me, just.... Here." The teenagers smoking on the stairs seem sketchier than usual. I say, "Thankyousomuch," without looking at Barton.

I hear, "Anytime," as I slide out the door. Upstairs, soaking in the shallow bathtub, I realize I didn't even give him enough time to try to kiss me, if he even wanted.

The day of the final exam, my whole body aches from not sleeping and it seems like every customer has some sort of issue: not enough napkins, the wrong brand of mustard, it's cold in the ladies' room, *are you sure this is diet—it doesn't taste like diet.*

I'm nervous, but as soon as I see the exam paper I feel okay. I've memorized all this, and the math isn't hard with a calculator. When I finish, everyone else is still bent over their papers. For a minute, I just watch heads, backs, arms, no faces. I wonder how everyone's doing, how they feel. I wonder if their feet hurt.

I recheck my answers until people start standing up and talking about going to some bar. I didn't know there was going to be a last-class party. Maybe I'm not invited. I put my notebook in my bag. I shouldn't be spending money anyway. "You're coming, aren't you?" Marina asks me. I guess I'm invited.

On the way over, I walk beside Barton. "How'd the test go?"

"Okay. Fine."

"Good. So you think you'll go on with tax stuff?"

"I think I could be good at it. And I want to help people."

"Isobel." He spreads his hands flat in front of him. "You have many gifts, but you need to concentrate your forces. Yeah, tax-preparers help but people don't necessarily appreciate it. You need to protect yourself...like at any job."

I think about Eva giving me the lunch shift that everyone fights over so I can go to class, taking tables for me when I fall behind, telling the grill guys not to yell at me.

At the pub, our waitress asks what we're celebrating.

"Wow, taxes."

It's funny to see all these classroom people under the beer-light glow. Barton's tie is looser now. I watch him sip his beer, answer Lachlan's questions about government spies, sign Stevey's EI form. Then he turns toward me. "Are you Greek, Isobel?"

"No...."

"The back-lah...back-lava? That pastry you said was Greek?"

"I'm a waitress in a Greek restaurant.

"Oh. Oh, that must be fun...talking to people, free food?" I can see myself reflected shiny and small in his glasses. I haven't had this beer since Montreal. It's Riley's brand, American, not my favourite but I can drink it. It smells like mid-afternoon, the old sofa we found on the curb, his voice arguing with the TV. I wonder if my phone is ringing right now.

The evening drags, but I stay. I'm covering Mara's lunch tomorrow, so I'm going to be sorry when I'm too tired to be polite when people change their orders, hate their orders, yell when they don't get what they didn't ask for. But I stay. When

I get back from the bathroom, there's a chair open next to Barton. I go sit there for a while.

We're the last two, which seems good. As we leave, Barton's talking about law school, how he studied all night for exams and flunked them anyway—"Sometimes, you just want to know you won't get anything wrong, you know?" He shakes his head as if something had fallen into his hair. "I just had to re-envision my path. I'll drive you home, right?" He's already walking toward the garage.

Barton finds my street from memory. He puts the car in park and turns the key. I don't think parking out here is legal, but maybe it's late enough. He's not staying, anyway. Probably. He asks, "You have fun tonight?"

I did. I liked the bad beer and the good waitress. I liked the way all Stevey's stories ended with "that fucker," and all of Ling's with "my husband thought I was crazy." I like having someone to talk about the night with after the night is over. I start to say, "Yeah," but Barton's already talking again.

"Great night, good class, a really good group. Very positive energy." He turns toward me, seatbelt still on. "How're your feet?"

I look down as if I'd forgotten they were there. "Not too bad. I got new insoles."

"For your sexy feet?" He says it too fast, like he's been waiting to say it, then laughs. Actually he just says, "Heh heh," like he's in a comic strip. He's fiddling with the gearshift now. I can see a hint of hair above his loose tie. I can see a glint of sweat on his forehead. It's a strange thought: I could kiss him if I wanted to. It'd be easy to lean over, arch my belly over the gearshift, reach my face toward his face.

He'd kiss me if I kissed him, I suddenly know it. He'd come upstairs if I let him, but he'd never ask. I could tell Mara and Eva. He could answer the phone the next time Riley called. If I wanted. But he would never lean across the gearshift. He'd let me take all the risks, make all the guesses. He's just some guy in this car.

He waits until I'm all the way on the sidewalk, just about to swing the door shut, before he reaches into his pocket for a card.

"This is…this is my card at the firm. I meant to pass these out at the end of class.… You should call me about a temp position in March. You'd be a great…great asset."

"Thank you." I want to be sure he knows I'm not thanking him for the card. "For the ride, and the class. And everything." I shut the door.

He mouths through the window, "Night, Iz."

"Night, Barton."

Upstairs I take my shoes and socks off. My feet leave little sweatprints on the cool tile as I cross the kitchen. The blast of freezer air feels good on my cheeks after sweating in the bar. The baklava box is damp, dinged up a little from being in my bag.

I imagine Riley sitting drunk in our old cold kitchen. I imagine Mara and her husband curled up with their tiny new baby. Then I imagine Barton getting home to his apartment in the basement of his parents' place. I take a baklava out of the box and put the card in its place, cup the pastry in my palms to thaw it. I know what Barton's kitchen looks like, because it's just like mine: the fridge and stove a funny orange from the seventies, tea towel draped over the oven handle, digital green clock on the stove. The only difference is my fridge is full of Greek foods Eva gave me, things with foreign characters I found at the Chinese grocery, takeout I'm saving, everything on sale. In Barton's kitchen, I know, there is only minute rice, Mr. Christie's cookies, tomato sauce in cans. Nothing that's hard to pronounce, or to fit into your mouth.

The House on Elsbeth

We got the house on Elsbeth for the summer because, one sleety day in April, Leah's stepfather backhanded her hard on the jaw. Ted's blow snapped her mouth shut mid-argument and made her bite straight through her tongue. Every moment we spent in the Elsbeth house that summer, we were living the story Leah told, all three of us imagining the arc of his hand stopping at her narrow face, a drop of blood continuing the arc across the room to spatter on the bone-white fridge. That's not a picture you can blink away, even if you never actually saw it.

On the skidding ride to the hospital, Leah wasn't quite the bitch she had a right to be; she never actually threatened to tell her mom, the cops, whatever. Nor was Ted the bastard he could have been. In the floaty white chaos of the ER, he told Leah maybe they'd get on better with more space between them. He'd give her one of his nicer properties, semi-detached, for half rent—if she could find friends to share it. A little dig, but nothing the limited bitch in Leah couldn't handle.

She didn't have to think, really, about who to ask. The three of us knew each other from our anthropology tutorial. Not well—to borrow a pencil or recognize a new tattoo, email class notes, that's all. But when Leah asked Lane and Tracy to live with her, it seemed like something we'd always been planning, even though we'd never had a conversation outside of that chalk-dusty classroom.

A punch in the face is a bad thing to have happen to you, but it's not so great, either, to hear through cheap wood panelling from the other half of the semi-house. Through a wall, we couldn't precisely identify the thud of flesh on flesh, but when that thud interrupts *I didn't, you said, you never, I hate*, when it's followed by the stagger-back of shoes and the crash of body into furniture, and then a wail, we knew what it was.

The first thud came a week after we'd moved into our half, at suppertime, dessert. Lane dropped his spoon on the kitchen tile and pictured the small woman with ragged red hair who lived next door. He imagined any blow, even from her spindly bearded husband, would toss her back quite far. Lane imagined himself—tall, with tennis-playing muscles—being tossed back. Less far, but still. He'd imagined this before. In front of the bathroom mirror, Lane and Tracy had both, separately, tried whipping their heads around, arching against the bathtub, wondering about angles and impact. Even Leah wasn't sure about the choreography, since there wasn't a mirror in her mother's kitchen. Nobody had a real clear picture.

There was a wail through the wall, short and sharp. Leah stopped picking the cherries out of the fruit cup and looked up at the wall, staring hard, as if she could melt it. She was thinking, not about pain, but about how it is to fall; to fall down and look up at someone bigger, someone who has just been proven stronger. A blow knocks you down, but it's the looking up afterwards that gets you.

Still, getting hit in the face is not the worst thing there is. It's not a killing blow. You can heal, recover dignity, get up from the floor. Leah could enunciate almost normally by then, in May. And the neighbours recovered even faster after that first blow: just a few minutes of sobs led to tender murmurs we couldn't make out. After even those quieted, we heard footsteps moving deeper into the house.

As the heels echoed away, Tracy picked up the spoon, covered with fluff and hair, and set it on the table. No-one was eating; no-one looked away from the bone-white wall.

When we felt sad, sometimes we played games. Leah sighed and said, "Pear," and Lane closed his eyes and stuck his

29

fingers into his fruitcup tin and picked out a translucent cube of pear. As he put the fruit in his mouth, he held out the cup above Tracy's head. Leah said, "Cherry," and Tracy shut her eyes and took a cherry, pink with cheap dye. She reached across the table to place it carefully on Leah's stitches.

Leah chewed and swallowed, licked at the juice. "Nothing irreparable." It sounded like a lie in her slurry voice, thick with healing, despite the silence behind the once-wailing wall.

Sometimes we saw the neighbours by the garbage cans, in the groceteria. They were small flabby people in slacks with elastic waists, but they took in their mail, mowed their lawn, carried their sacks of empties to the Beer Store. They seemed functional.

On our side of the wall, things moved slowly, and the tins and bottles piled up. We couldn't get much done in that dark, hot little house. The wood panelling absorbed the heat and breathed it out at us. We thought about trying to make the weather cooler, we wondered if we could have. We decided to save our energy for bigger problems.

Lane had the most energy. He had a summer class, and mornings he shot like a spitball down the stairs from the bathroom, shower-damp through his shirt, white-blond hair slicked translucent to his skull. Some of his freshness dissolved in the living-room.

We all slept on the floor downstairs, where it was cooler, and Tracy and Leah would still be there, sprawled like starfish. It was really too hot to touch but somehow bare legs always tangled on the thin grey rug. Leah's waitress blue-threaded pale legs, Tracy's tanned and muscular from her landscaping job, sapped Lane's desire for his Micro Economics, even though his own legs—not so pale, but not so tan—had been in the twist just twenty minutes before. When we closed our eyes, it felt as if we were all still touching.

Our sense of each other was getting stronger and stronger. Even back in Cultural Anthro, stacking Maslow's needs into need triangles, we could feel the current. Leah's pin-straight hair would rise and crackle when Lane or Tracy brushed past her. Or Lane would suddenly taste mint in his empty mouth and look across the classroom to see Leah or Tracy crumpling a gum wrapper. Or Tracy would think of an answer to a test question and then, before she could write it down, realize that it was not hers but Lane's or Leah's. She'd shake her head if it wasn't right, then watch the careful erasing. We all always felt the urge to stand too close, to brush arms, shoulders, bellies, without a word to say to each other. So it felt natural to live together, to try to get as close as possible for all the hours in the day. On the morning in question, Leah was zebra-faced with last night's makeup and Tracy was eating dry Reese's Peanut-Butter Cereal, puff by puff, without raising her head from her pillow. The heat had nearly totalled us.

There was a slam from the wall, wood against metal.

Lane sighed and stood still. "I gotta go to class."

Leah nodded, dark hair sliding into her mouth. She spit it out. "It may be too hot to go to class, Lane. It may be too hot to go on at all." Her voice was still slow, but no longer slurred, not at all. This was nearly July, and she was healing fast.

"Maybe we should spend more time in the yard." Lane was thinking about how it would feel to flunk a summer course, one he'd paid for, and he didn't want to think about that. "Maybe we'd feel cooler in the air. Is that barbeque still there? I know how to grill."

He sat down on the couch and Tracy squirmed up to lean on him. Her skull felt heavy against his thigh. She nibbled on another peanut-butter ball. "It's out there. And I applaud this burst of enthusiasm." She was thinking about how she had to leave for work and she didn't know if she could face the subway, or putting on clothes.

The voices on the other side of the wall didn't separate into a man and a woman. A single snarl of anger, braiding alto and tenor until the blow fell again, again again.

We squirmed at the cartoon *bonk* of a head on wall. It sounded like a dropped shoe. But it wasn't. Tracy stopped chewing. Through the wall, we imagined we could hear recrimination, apology, the smack of freezer door. Then we imagined the hissing sting of ice on a hot bruise. Lane and Tracy looked hard at Leah's dirty face, watching for any pain that could be comforted.

Leah slipped off the couch and walked toward the far wall. "A barbeque would be fun. We've got chicken and buns, and...we'll play Frisbee." She laughed, her nose bending against the wall. The other side was fading into tears, mutters. "Tomorrow my stepdad's coming to pick up the rent."

It was hard to believe that it was the end of June already, or that it hadn't always been June. Tracy slid her head off Lane's thigh. Freed, Lane stood and went to touch Leah's shoulder, bend his nose against the wall, too. "Does he own that place, too?" We all knew he was going to ask, but actually mentioning the neighbours aloud was startling.

"Not relevant. But yes. Tonight," Leah said firmly. "Barbecue. Okay."

You're fuckin' shirts can't get dry the humidity you don't listen never listen fuck fuck fuck

Lane and Tracy were in the backyard after work. The radio said it was too hot and smoggy to be outside, but that was assuming you had some indoor place to go that was air-conditioned and didn't smell like old beer and dust. The shiny black Frisbee was by the back door, waiting. Lane had managed to get the coals lit, though the burns on his hand itched and tingled. Tracy was lying on the dead grass, still starfish sprawling, counting the singed hairs on the back of Lane's hand across the yard. She hadn't showered after work and Lane could feel the slick sweat on her nose and neck. He picked up a glass from the ground and went to kneel beside her.

"You should drink. It's 38 out here, the radio said."

"We're 38 degrees, too. People are. Neat." Tracy kept her eyes closed. They could both see the sun shining through blood vessels in her eyelids.

"C'mon. Delicious grape Tang."

I've never lying your mother my mother my ass you take the recycling your mother I hate

Tracy took the glass and rested it at the vee of her ribs, hands folded around it like a funeral bouquet. "Where's Leah?"

"Working. Or on her way home from work...." Lane squinted at what remained of the sun. "Yeah, she'll be back soon."

Clouds were starting to gather in the west, where you could almost see the intention of sunset. Old Elvis Costello on the radio. Leah came in from the street gate in her black uniform, each leg outlined in sweat on her skirt.

"What's up?" Lane stood and watched her fiddle with the gate, the rub of her damp skirt against the hair on his thighs.

"One of the sous-chefs ditched and they put me in the kitchen. Fuckers. I cut my hand dicing onions and got burnt off the toaster." She came closer and shoved her hands toward Lane's face. Her fingers were long, skinny and pale. Each knuckle was cross-hatched with tiny cuts or crusted with a larger scrape. Across the veiny back of the left, a long cut bled a mirror heart line through a Barbie-flesh bandaid.

"Okay?" He pointed at the cut.

She flopped onto the grass next to Tracy. "Cuise wanted me to get it looked at, but I didn't have cab fare and bleeding on TTC...you know?"

Land reached down and pressed his burns against hers. "You want some Tang?"

"Sit with me a minute first. Tracy's asleep."

"No." Tracy opened her eyes. "Hello, Leah."

Lane sat down, draping himself over Leah's sticky back.

Tracy sat up. "Hey, the sky is purple." She dropped her head into Leah's lap.

"Ah, the puppy pile." Leah patted Tracy's head with her less-injured hand.

Clashing voices from the other side of the house, again. Again and again and again. The air was heavy with rage and the possibility of rain.

"I hate it," Lane said after a minute. Thunder rumbled, not too far off.

Leah nodded.

Tracy said, "Maybe we should do something. About that. Them."

Just once your part I mean jesus you expect nine to five the weekends really jesus

Lane said, "*Can* we do something? I mean, we don't...."

"C'mon. We can."

We were quiet for a moment. The neighbours were not quiet.

Fucking fucking fuck

"What time is Ted coming tomorrow, Leah?"

"Early." A slammed door. Then more voices. "But we've got it under control, right? So it doesn't matter."

Never see it comin' just like bitch and this weather one time in the now that I'm making

"Next door?"

Leah stared at the fence. "We not gonna mention it, are we?"

Hurting me hurting dinner on the table what bastard responsibility bacon totally hate

"Ask him to ask them...."

"Ask them what? Please stop what?...everything?"

The fence was painted pudding-brown. At the base was a moat of dirt, which the heat had bleached blond and shattered like glass.

It wasn't clear who said it. Maybe we all said it: "Please stop hitting her?"

He hit her. We were too far to hear the blow, and there was no cry. In the sudden silence, though, it seemed obvious.

The sweat had dried off Leah and her clothes hung free. She was still staring at the fence. Tracy curved her body over Leah's, chest on spine, heart on heartbeat.

The clouds were building. The air smelled like grilled chicken, brown sugar and bourbon, dead grass, sweat and botanical products radiating off our bodies. We were listening through the steamy air to a murmur that, deep in the house, was building again. The woman's voice was not young, gravelly, enraged. The man's was higher, more hysterical. We were losing more words now, but they seemed all one syllable, *bang* like hammer strokes, shattering. *Bangbangbang,* the woman's voice, *I want, you did, this house, I hate, stop.* Then the man's voice. Then both, again. Then silence, then the crash of china and another crash of voices.

Lane got up and went to poke a fork into a scorched chicken breast and flip it. A small flame blazed, then died.

"I don't feel too good," Tracy said to the sky. She pulled back from Leah.

"Eh, you don't look too good, either," Leah said, turning, reaching to clutch Tracy's hand. She looked down at their twined fingers, all the cuts and dirty bruises and rings between them. Shriek of children, happier neighbours elsewhere.

"Nice, nice of you." Tracy stuck out her Tang-purple tongue.

Leah laughed and flicked hers fast, out and in.

Tracy breathed. "Hey, your tongue's healed. You don't even have a scar."

A shout that sounded like a parting shot, and then the bang-back of a screen door, the stomp of shoes on grass. The last cloud finally floated over the platinum sun and winked it out. A rustle, someone in the next garden, *him.*

"Where do scars go when they go away?"

"Nowhere. It's gone."

"Nothing goes nowhere."

The thunder rumbled again, closer, deeper.

Lane poked at a chicken burger, burnt on one side, raw on the other. He hated the pink of the raw.

Tracy was trying to dig in under the grass. She didn't like the feel of the dry dirt. She wanted it to be mud.

"It doesn't matter," Leah said, wanting one punch not to matter. Ted was coming by in the morning, and she wanted to like him again. "I get hit in the face once, we get Montreal rent in Toronto." He'd probably want a cup of coffee, minutes together, minutes and minutes in the hot ugly kitchen, and she couldn't like him again. "What happened to me is not what's happening...there." Silence from the next yard. Leah thought of her stepfather's pinched face when he'd been working too hard, the strain lines and the smile lines around his eyes. "For her...."

Lane tried to put chicken breast onto a bun, dropped it in the grass, picked it up and burned his fingers with an audible hiss, dropped it again, finally got it with the spatula.

"I'll eat that one," he said. We could all feel the burn blisters forming on his index finger, but he just set the plate down and reached for the next one. He looked over when Tracy said, "Can I touch?"

She knelt beside Leah and tapped her on the right corner of her mouth. Leah shrugged and put her tongue out again: lizard-long and ham-pink, cracked like drought soil, spit bubbles and pasty tastebuds. Tracy stared, Lane stared, even Leah was looking, her dark eyes crossed.

It was late afternoon and our yard was night-time dark and we could hear the neighbour's hoe smacking soil. Tracy rubbed her index finger on her shirt but it still looked dirty grey. Leah didn't flinch when she touched her. Under the rough pad of Tracy's finger, Leah's tongue felt silky wet, trembling faintly. A tongue is all muscle. Lane set down the plate and came close, watching the pale of Tracy's fingernail stroke up and down. He knelt on Leah's other side and raised his right index finger, blistered and meat-greasy. He waited for Leah's affirmative blink before putting the bubble of blister next to Tracy's finger. Hers was cooler, but both brushed gently where tooth had slammed at hand on jaw, where the scar should have been. But there was no scar.

Then the rain hit our backs.

We ate in the rain and the echo of thunder, the buns melting to sponge, Tracy's hair slick on her shoulders, Leah's makeup black rivers on her cheeks. Lane ate his burger and then half of Tracy's and then he picked up the Frisbee. Its plastic lightning bolts were far thicker than the true stuff in the sky, shellacked glossy and still. Real lightning rents the world.

We fanned into a triangle to play, flawless throws and catches despite the pounding-down water, despite Lane's his burnt finger, Leah's cut hand, Tracy's rasping breath. The small clonk of a thumb hooking the edge of the Frisbee soothed, despite the weight of sodden clothes clinging, the weight of what we were doing.

After 30 throws, ten each without a miss, the air was full of lightning, spiderthreads of white heat. It was raining only in our yard; the neighbour gardened on, the *chink* of rake against dead-dry dirt.

Lane nodded, and Leah lofted the thing up over Tracy's idle hand, and the fence. At that moment, a crack of thunder, an arc of light flickering into the corn, hot and sharp. A hiss of fire, then a heavy body falling, then nothing.

The walls were silent, the fence was silent. We bowed our heads a moment.

Then we went around front and across to the neighbours' dry driveway. Leah knocked on the door to the other half of

37

our house. Dripping and not invited in, we told the woman what we'd seen over the fence, or hadn't seen but knew was there. She didn't ask why we were dripping. We went to the garden to show her the Frisbee one row of corn away from his open hand. After the silence had passed, we pressed our wet bodies against each other's, and then hers, as she wept.

Tech Support

I. TECH

Clint stayed under Ursula's desk, staring at the green glow of the power-bar light. After a while her yelling and spike-heeled stomp on the carpet ceased, as if she was thinking things over. Clint didn't need to see to know her hands were fisted on hips, legs planted wide. He thought he could feel her glare on his spine while he hunched over the CPU, fiddling, not really working. Finally she hammered off down the hall.

The screws on the old adapter were bent and wouldn't turn smoothly. It didn't help that he was coming at it from an odd angle, jammed under the desk, and that his fingers were slick with sweat. He heard rustling above him, but kept on with the screws—Ursula wasn't capable of making so little noise and no-one else was out for his blood. When he'd finally gotten the broken plug off, it only took a few seconds to put on the new one. The shiny puffin emblem caught the light that filtered down between the desk and the wall.

When he pulled back to sit in front of the desk, Anna was sitting on the floor next to him. Her ankles were tucked under her thighs, a mug in each fist. She held out the left one, pale beige, the way he liked it. "This one's yours."

He took the scalding ceramic in his hand without thinking, and had to set it down on the carpet to grab the handle. He sniffed. "You make this?"

"Had to. Luddock's hungover."

She took a sip and smiled forcefully, like an advertisement, so he did, too. The coffee was thin and opaque and nutty— good, for office coffee.

"'S great," Clint said. "I guess Ursula misses out on this."

"What was that all about?"

Sitting on the floor across from her, Clint could quite clearly see Anna's panties. They were navy. He tried to concentrate on her face. "What?"

"Ursula. I heard her come storming out of here."

"Ursula storms to the bathroom. You're working up here today?"

"Just an hour or so. A couple new monitors in Creative. But what happened...?"

"Oh. I. I wasn't.... She thinks I work too slow. She wanted you, I believe."

"Ah. This was the monitor adapter?"

"Yep." He opened his damp palm to reveal the dented plug and warped screws.

"Well, that's ruined. What'd she do, kick it?" Anna grinned into her mug.

Clint didn't smile. "Looks like." He pitched the thing over his left shoulder as he stood up and was pleased to hear it ping into the wastebasket. Then he collapsed into Ursula's ergonomic desk chair and started checking screen settings. "Fucking Ursula."

Anna pulled her cup away from her lips. "Don't let her get to you, Clint."

Clint kept his eyes on the screen—the resolution was off and he wanted to reset it and reboot before Ursula stormed back. "She said I'm a worthless Tech tool."

"She's got Dallas next week," Anna said quickly. "She's pressed." Anna gazed at his coffee cup. "Don't you want this?"

"It's too strong to drink fast." He reached down and hooked the mug handle with his left hand, still mouse-clicking with his right. "Luddock's got to get it together."

"Buck up," Anna said softly, face still pointing toward the floor.

Ursula's computer wallpaper was a Rothko painting, bright rectangles dotted with icons. It was hard to tell how the screen read on it. "This look all right to you?"

"It looks like a sunset." She stood up then, pressed her hand down her thighs, smoothing her skirt.

He hit Restart and stood up, too. He wanted to be taller than her again. "You think we should have an intervention for Luddock?"

She slouched onto her left hip. "Yeah."

"I want another coffee. You coming?" He extended his arm and she twined hers around it. They went everywhere like this, from cubes to assignment to lunch to elevator. Anna was just an arm-linker. People made assumptions, but Anna didn't notice and Clint didn't mind. He'd learned to take what he could get.

Luddock was sitting cross-legged on Clint's desk. "Whatja fuck up?"

"I didn't. What did you get into last night?" Clint put his mug down, rolled his chair back, sat. A rubber chicken was lying on his filing cabinet. He hadn't put it there.

A raised-eyebrow leer. Luddock started unfolding his stick-figure legs. His left loafer tapped Clint on the sternum. "Sorry. I heard Ursula shrieking at you."

"No big thing. She's just—"

"Madly in hate with you, I know. Could be a cover for lust."

"She doesn't even know my name. She has no specific emotions related to me. She just likes to yell."

"Yeah, yeah. If she makes a move, I say screw the corporate ladder..." Luddock went into his own cube but kept talking, the sound undisturbed by the fabric wall "...and go for it. Worth any Tech job, hellion like that."

"I'm glad you costed it. Listen, what time are we meeting the cab tomorrow?"

"Six, as discussed." The squawk of the springs in Luddock's pre-ergonomic chair.

"So early? We're gonna be sitting around with social committee."

"You're too new—you've never seen this place get non-denominationally down to celebrate the birth of Christ. The

41

open bar gets less open every year. This time it's only the cocktail hour, not after dinner. Cheap bastards."

"It's to keep people from driving drunk."

"You buy me a car, then we'll worry about that. Trust me, the free dinner does not pay for dry-cleaning, let alone the cab."

"And...Trinity?" Clint couldn't really say the name without blinking a couple times, it seemed so likely that Luddock had made her up.

"She's driving from work. She's worried about traffic making her late."

"It's cool if you don't have a date, you know. I haven't got a date, Anna hasn't—half the department's stag."

"She'll *be* there, she might just be late." Luddock just went back to clicking and Clint rolled back to his station too, and there was silence and they both got three-quarters of an hour of work done before Luddock said, "Anna's not bringing someone?"

"You knew that. She said it before the Oracle meeting on Thursday."

"Yeah. But, I thought she was, like, kidding."

Clint stared hard at the cloth wall that separated his desk from Luddock's. "Yeah, weird." Anna and Ursula. Weird. Clint wondered, if he told Luddock, would he be crude about it, or would he have something wise to say. Luddock was often unexpectedly wise, and often not. And Clint didn't know if he could even tell the story, if it even was a story.

There was the click of three or four keystrokes, another chair creak, then, "She's not...she's going with *us,* right? She's not going *with you,* right?"

Clint sent pages to print before setting his forehead on the mousepad. "Yeah."

"Ah." Resettling of weight. "*A priori* it didn't seem likely, but I thought I'd ask."

Already a week ago, just a glimpse. Still the memory

42

unfurled inside his eyelids like an epic: in the parking garage, in the stairwell just above Parkade C, he saw Anna's hip pressed awkwardly against the railing and Ursula's fingers against Anna's jaw. Just a moment, before Ursula raised her eyes to his face, and made him skitter up the stairs.

"I'm gonna go bug her while she's on helpdesk. Wanna come, Clinty?"

Clint knew that Anna was probably waiting for him to come ask about the rubber chicken, so he didn't. He put it into the drawer with the other toys that had turned up in Tech: waterguns, Beanie Babies, Kinder Surprises, Nerf balls. He wondered if he would get any more if he stopped asking about them.

"Nah, I'm gonna work on the Firefox presentation."

The rumble of chair wheels stopped. "No-one cares about Firefox, Clinty."

"They care about pop-ups. I can just do a quick PowerPoint—"

"Clint, Clint, Clint. No. One. *Cares*. *No-one* is going to switch, because it's too much effort. It's too much effort to listen to the presentation."

Clint opened his notes on consumer-protection features. "It's going to save aggravation in the long run...." A rubber band shot over the partition. "Luddock, you know I'm right."

"You're right, you're right. I'll get you a notarized letter to that effect if you don't disrupt the meeting trying to make things slightly more efficient for, like, four people—"

A Pearl eraser tapped Clint on the neck and half a dozen paperclips rained onto his hair. One fell into his mouth and he had to blow it out before he could speak. "Hey—"

"—and *piss off* everyone else in the meeting to the point where they're jerks to *all* of Tech for the next *month*, 'cause they can't remember—" a tissue box knocked Clint's jar of pens onto the floor "—which of those fuckheads made that *useless* presentation."

Clint let pens roll onto the floor and started writing about tabbed browsing.

"Clint, are you listening to me? Clint, if you make that presentation, so help me god, I will wrestle you to the floor before you get past the first pixilated fade. Clint?"

Clint gazed at the air above his screen, thinking about pixilated fades and the futility of PowerPoint. Something cracked hard across the bridge of his nose. *"Jesus!"*

"Clint? Just close the file, okay? Close it and work on something that matters."

"You threw a calculator at me, Luddock?" All kinds of extra *B*s were inserting themselves into his speech—*Yoob threwb ab....* His screen had gone static. So had the walls and air.

"I've got a desk set, kid. I've been here longer than you. I can take you *down.*"

A blotch of sunset red appeared on the beige desk. "I'm down." *Ib dowb.*

"What?"

"Calculators are hard, Luddock. I'm wounded."

"Ah, shut the fuck—"

Clint stood up. His hands were shaking and his upper lip was hot, but it seemed vital that Luddock not know the extent of the damage. "Back in a sec, bud." He went toward the bathroom the way that didn't pass Luddock's cube.

The hallway lights buzzed, which they had never done before. The office was really a bit too nice for that sort of thing, so Clint thought maybe he'd sustained a brain injury through his nose. He wanted to put his hot face against the cold bathroom mirror.

Ursula was a parody of her own name: tall and skinny as a flagpole, unbrushed curls the colour of halogen light. She wore a brilliant green suit that day, no makeup. Her face went bond-paper white when she saw Clint. She even stopped striding. Her forward momentum had been such that her shoulders lurched forward after her feet stopped.

"Jesus, Clint. What the fuck is this?"

Clint could feel his blood pounding in his nose like another heart. He wondered if she could see it. "You know my name?"

Ursula's enormous raspberry lips were working in and out very fast. "I know your name. And I'm gonna get you some ice. I'm really not that much of a bitch, you know. That much." Clint could hear her heels *pock*ing toward the kitchen. The hall spun like a windmill blade. He staggered into the men's room.

The mirror held no good news. A Yosemite-Sam moustache of blood. The stuff was a fake-looking red in the white-tile room, like slasher-movie ketchup. When he tried to swipe his sleeve across his face he got blood in his eye. Tears mixed with the blood. Clint's stomach was starting to buck and weave. He hung over the sink and watched his blood dilute in the tap drip. Tipping his head forward seemed to make the blood flow faster. It was too thin, too, Clint thought. Too thin and too much, couldn't be right. He tried to remember what he used to do about nosebleeds in elementary school, besides cry.

The door swung open and Ursula burst in, frost-crusted Lean Cuisine box in her hand, her hair standing up like an electric shock, stunning as usual. In the summer, one of the interns had had such a crush on her he'd had to quit.

Ursula's heels made the same hammering sound in the men's room they did anywhere else. Clint wondered why he was surprised. She pressed the chicken primavera box across the hard bone of Clint's nose.

"Tip back. And press the ice. Well, there wasn't any ice."

Facing the ceiling, Clint tasted blood sliding down the back of his throat, like a salty penny. He tried to clear his throat and gagged, spraying red onto the picture of chicken. When he got his breath, Clint said, "Thanks for letting me bleed on your lunch."

45

"It isn't mine. I just found it in the freezer." Ursula seemed deflated by this admission, sagging back against the sink, getting blood and damp on her skirt.

"Thank you for stealing someone else's lunch for me."

Ursula's laugh was like a seal bark, echoing off porcelain toilets.

Clint smiled, then winced, then stopped.

"It hurts?"

Icicles had started to stab back into Clint's sinuses, but he shook his head. A blood drop hit Ursula's left breast. She looked down at it and her pink nostrils flared. "Stop moving."

Clint stopped breathing.

"You need to give it time to clot."

Clint started to nod and then stopped. There was a tiny curve across Ursula's hips where her skirt bunched like the knot on a bow-tie, a fan of wrinkles. Under the fluorescent bathroom bulbs her white face looked funeral beautiful.

"You need to stay out of people's way, Clint. You piss people off." Ursula was running the blade of her right stiletto up and down over her left calf, shredding her stocking. She didn't seem to notice.

His chin and neck were going crunchy with dried blood. When he tipped his jaw to see her, Clint could feel it flake over his jugular. "I didn't tell anyone. I mean, I didn't yet and I won't. So...." He was thinking about how warm Anna was, if you brushed her shoulder, and how Ursula looked hypothermic.

"What?" The heel *pock*ed back down onto the tile. "Is that a threat?"

"No. How could it be?"

Her hands were long and full of ocean-blue veins that pulsed as she gripped the countertop. She'd put one of those icicle hands along Anna's cinnamon skin, brushing her hair back, caressing her face. It was impossible he could've seen mouths and eyes in the exhaust-fume gloom, but his mind extrapolated, filled in gaps. A narrow hand stilling Anna's chattering mouth. Ursula leaning over, Anna's head tilting to the side. Or tilted by Ursula's firm hand. Anna, anyway, under Ursula's slim shadow.

"I just wanted to tell you I won't tell, so you can stop trying to scare me so I won't. Because I *already* won't." Clint could see himself in the mirror, head back under the white box, The veins in his throat were as blue as those in Ursula's hands. "And I'm already scared. But that has nothing to do with it."

Ursula brushed her corkscrews in no particular direction. "What do you mean?"

Clint had lost thread and risked straightening his neck to see her face. He hadn't stopped shaking, but he was getting used to it.

She was looking down sorrowfully at the scraps of her nylons. She bent to tug at the fabric. Clint heard the threads snapping. When she straightened up, she looked hard at Clint's swollen nose. "Do you mean, you being scared of me has nothing to do with whether you'll gossip about me and Anna?"

Breathing through his mouth made his teeth dry. Clint had to swallow even just to say, "Yeah."

Ursula raised her skinny eyebrows toward her hairline. "Lucky Anna. I guess." Then she leaned back on the counter, reaching a hand underneath her skirt. Clint could see her hand moving like a green ghost. "Your nose...is it broken?"

"No."

With the pantyhose around her knees, Ursula was stepping out of her shoes, concentrating mainly on them and not on Clint. "Your voice sounds nasal. It could be broken. I'll take you to the hospital if you want."

"No."

"No, it's not broken, or no, you don't want me to take you?" Barelegged, she slid back into her shoes and straightened, carefully centering herself back onto her spikes. "Wait, don't answer that. Don't ever ask me for anything. That is the only thing I'd do for you." Ursula peered at him, her eyes enormous and gleaming blue as her veins. "You don't know shit, you know that, right? I could paint walls with what you don't know."

Clint could smell her spearmint chewing gum over the urinals and chlorine cleanser and Alfredo sauce. He was startled to realize his nose was functioning again, that it would be okay. He could see his face in the mirror over Ursula's shoulder, the rivers of caked blood on his neck and collar and smeared up to his left eye. Cream sauce had just started to thaw and seep out of the swollen, crumpled box. The first drop landed just to the left of the fly.

"I don't know shit," he said. There wasn't really much else to say, or time to say it before the scheduling meeting.

Ursula seemed to be considering his honesty before she nodded, one quick jerk of the chin. She turned toward the door. As she opened the door she tried to toss the flesh-toned wad of pantyhose over her shoulder into the bin, but it slid down the stainless-steel onto the tile and stray crumpled paper towels. Her shoes were quiet as she strode out.

II. SUPPORT

As it turned out, Trinity was not only real but beautiful. All spangled green dress, upswept hair, lipgloss smile—all for Luddock, with three inches of wrist and ankle jutting out of his brother's suit, a row of open-bar cocktails in front of him. Luddock introduced Clint with a sweeping arm flourish. "This is Clint. This morning I hit him with a calculator. Now he's plotting my death."

"I'm Trinity." She had a wide, white-toothed smile, a firm handshake.

"Welcome to our Holiday Celebration, Trinity." *Trinity*

had sounded so made-up. Clint had expected to spend the evening listening to Luddock pretend to talk on his turned-off cell phone, telling this imaginary girl it didn't matter if she was late, later, missed the party.

"Hello, Clint. Oh, little Christmas tree centrepieces. How nondenominational. Please don't kill my date." Her gaze flipped away without waiting for an answer.

Clint glanced around the ballroom, too. He spotted Ursula alone by the bar in a long black gown, wild white-blond curls. Anna was nowhere in sight. His nose throbbed.

They settled down to drink Luddock's hoard of drinks ("Never know when they're going to get even chintzier!") and mock the decorations and wait for Anna. There were half a dozen tables of IT, but the support team was cornered by the kitchen door. Sitting down, it was hard to see the bar, or the creative table where Ursula was seated.

Anna's voice drifted from behind him. "There is a stranger in our midst." Everybody turned. "I'm Anna. You must be Trinity." She reached out a hand. The day before, she'd bet Clint a granola bar that Luddock got her name from *The Matrix*.

"Hello, Anna. Luddock says you're my main competition."

"He's lying to make you jealous." Anna flopped into the chair beside Clint.

"Is it working?"

"Oh, I'm furious." Trinity leaned over and bit Luddock just beside the Adam's apple. Luddock winced, and smiled.

Anna wore a blue dress, shiny blue and wide-necked, revealing clavicles, sternum, initial rises of breasts. When she reached out her right hand to shake Trinity's, the neck shifted, clinging to the right side of her neck and baring her left shoulder. There was a flash of white-blond hair moving from bar to table. Clint caught it; Anna, as far as he could tell, didn't.

Clint had anticipated a miserable Holiday Celebration:

49

chafing in his necktie, squirming in humiliation for Luddock's imaginary girl, averting his gaze every time Anna looked at Ursula, making sure Ursula never noticed him at all. Blood still clotting at the edges of his nostrils, pounding migraine. But over the stacked Portobello salad, Trinity said, "You know, certain people in the sixties thought orgies would have become de rigueur by now, replacing parties like this entirely. Isn't it weird that after all this time, we're still repressed? This evening doesn't even have orgiastic *elements.*"

The whole table was entertained right through the chicken supreme. Anna never even looked toward Ursula, who was silent and grim, her fork neatly by the side of her plate.

Dessert was a wafer cup filled with mango mousse. Luddock tried his first, and quickly spat mousse back into his cup, wiped his mouth with his sleeve. Trinity stared. "It tasted like toothpaste."

"The party favour is chocolate truffles," she said. "Eat those."

"I ate mine at cocktail hour."

"Me, too. Clint?"

"Eaten."

"I'm keeping mine as a souvenir!" Anna hugged her purse, the same fabric as her dress. Clint wondered if she'd made them herself.

Luddock pushed his chair back. "You know, some hotshots have *left* already, without their free truffles. C'mon, Clinty, before the servers get them."

Trinity scooted closer to Luddock. "Actually, I was hoping we could have...an early night."

"Oh?" He swung around. "You want to go?"

"Well, unless you really wanted to stay...?"

Luddock's eyebrows shot up. "No. *No.* What the lady says goes. Let's go."

They went. Clint and Anna, shoulders brushing in silence, were the only two at the table—the rest of the Tech proles long gone or drunkenly doing some dance with arm motions. Anna was deconstructing the centrepiece, watching Ursula's bare pale shoulders and the long curve of her back. Clint watched Anna watching, her pink mouth slightly ajar. She twisted two pine twigs together. Ursula folded her matchstick arms below her breasts, glared at the dancers. Anna only shrugged when Clint announced, "Right back."

He'd noticed a couple of fullish wine bottles had been abandoned on the next table. Finance. Clint went over to the empty table and plucked them from among the stained napkins and truffle boxes. Those were empty, for some reason. No-one spoke to him; he didn't know anyone outside Tech. Anna was stuck with him. Poor Anna.

When he got back to the table, Anna had built a little man out of bits of greenery from the centrepiece. Clint had three wine-bottles clutched in his hands.

Anna looked at him, bright-faced. "You planning on a long night?"

"Never hurts to be prepared."

She thrust out her glass. "Red, please."

Someone asked Ursula to dance; Clint was sure Anna saw. Ursula uncrossed her arms and held them out stiffly, her face trying to animate. At that moment, it was hard for Clint to believe in Ursula's attractiveness, that the man in the tux (probably not rented) could want anything with her other than the professional connection.

Clint sloshed wine into their glasses as they watched the couple spin. Ursula's skirt sloshed like the wine. One revolution, she faced the Tech table, and Clint saw her big cyan eyes rest on Anna, and for a moment she was gorgeous.

He drank his medicine-flavoured wine and turned to Anna's lovelit face. "So——"

She startled, dropped her gaze and her smile. "How's your nose?"

"It's not broken, I keep telling you, it just looks bad."

"Luddock is *such* a fucker." She smiled a little, but it wasn't very realistic. She looked again at the dance-floor. Something ABBA was playing.

Then Trinity reappeared by the bar, breathless and flushed. She caught Clint's eye and waved like a semaphore. Clint stood up slowly.

"Hmm?" Anna purred as if waking.

Clint pointed at Trinity, and gathered the bottles.

Anna got up. "I wonder what's wrong."

Clint shrugged. "Only one way to find out." He extended his arm toward her, the hand without the wine, and Anna hooked on, warm and close. Trinity met them on the edge of the dance-floor, now radiating Steve Winwood. Ursula was at the bar, but Anna focused on Trinity's cold-flushed face.

"D'you guys know how to jimmy open a window?" she blurted as soon as they got within earshot.

"Maybe...not really.... Why?"

"We were—" Trinity's face flushed even more. If Clint hadn't liked her before, he would've now. "I started the car but there was snow over the windows, so Luddock got out to brush, but he wasn't, wasn't *doing* it right. He was leaving streaks."

Clint nodded—that seemed plausible.

"So I got out, to show him."

"And locked your keys in the car," Anna added.

"With the motor running! We've been trying to break in for twenty minutes. Luddock's standing guard. Do you have *any* ideas?" Trinity put hand to forehead, faux-swoon, but she looked miserable under her irony.

"No, but we'll come help. Or look. Or just stand around your car with you."

"Absolutely," said Anna, and did not look behind her.

"Oh, thank you," Trinity wailed. "I'll go wait with Luddock."

Trinity rushed off. Clint pulled his mouth to one side.

"She's awfully grateful. I wonder if she realizes what tech support actually does."

Anna shrugged. "I think it's a moral support thing."

They unchecked their coats and stole a hanger and went into the snowthick parking-lot. Clint felt like he had won something: he was still near Anna, yet not listening to "Jingle Bell Rock" in sad silence. The wet snow felt perfect on his face after the hot dry party. His nose didn't hurt much at all.

Anna was trying to unbend her hanger as they headed for Luddock's headlamp silhouette. She walked awkwardly in through the slush, even though her shoes were low, sensible. The big snowflakes wet her hair, curling it around her face. She might've been cold, but Clint knew she'd never take out her toque from deep in her big parka pocket. The toque had a pompom on the tip, and said Edmonton Oilers. She wore it on the way to work, but took it off before she came near the office. If Clint caught the right morning bus, he saw her with her head dipped over a book, the blue pompom bobbing with the bumps. If he sat with her, she'd be glad, but she'd take off the hat and fluff her hair, as if he were anyone. As if he had to be impressed. He almost never let her know he was there.

Luddock threw up his arms at their approach, cawing, "Clint, wine, Anna, a hanger! Thank *God.*"

Clint set the bottles in a snowbank, except one. Anna handed Luddock her almost-straightened hanger. "Now what?"

More snow fell.

Luddock slumped forward. "Everyone knows that wire hangers open car doors but—let me guess—no-one actually knows *how*, right?"

"Right," said Anna, sadly.

"We're hardly car thieves," said Trinity, more hysterical than sad.

Clint blinked snowflakes off his eyelashes. "Pull out the rubber at the bottom of the window and slip the hanger in above the lock. Use the tip to move the tumblers."

Everyone looked at the hanger with new affection; at Clint too. "All right...rubber part...." Luddock turned to the car, muttering.

Clint had no idea how to jimmy a lock, but what he'd said seemed logical. He heard the scrape of wire on glass and took a sip of wine. It really was cheap stuff.

Trinity went over to the snowdrift. "It's like an open bar!" She plucked a bottle. "Thanks, Clinty."

"Clinty is *my* name for him. Clinty is my creation!" Luddock yelled, thrashing at the window. "Anna, come try this. Your delicate hands will do better."

Trinity glared. "*My* hands are delicate."

"She's the best—" Luddock held up his own giant hand "—at some things. You're best at others." He handed Anna the wire.

Trinity didn't smile, but Luddock just kissed her mouth and took her wine.

"Don't worry. Tech support can fix anything."

Anna froze. "We're not *fix*ing it. A lock that's locked is working fine. We're trying to *break* it."

"Well, you can do that, too."

Trinity reached for the wine but Luddock pulled back. "You can't drink too much. I don't know how to drive."

Trinity spun toward the car, laughing, sort of. Luddock threw his arm around Clint, bottle bruising his biceps. They started walking down the aisle of cars. "Holding up, old man?"

"I'm all right."

"You're dying. Why are you dying? It's not your car."

"I'm not—"

"Ya *are.*"

"*Fuck!*" Anna's voice, quite clear. Something about the snow made voices carry.

"I'm fine.... You don't drive?"

54

"You don't date." Couples moved in the distance, arguing or cuddling. "Everyone knows you want Anna. Do something already."

"She doesn't want anything done."

"Chickenshit."

"She's not into it." Clint looked up. The sky was starless, brown: low clouds reflecting suburban light. The snow was thickening, but it didn't seem cold, just damp. He felt sweaty beneath his coat, suit, halo of wine.

"You haven't told her *you're* into it."

"That's not the problem." He almost blew his stupid secrets, for the warm weight of Luddock's arm and the ozone smell of snowflakes and how much better a person Clint was than Ursula.

"You two should be together. Look at her."

They turned to the still-sealed car. Anna was scrambling up onto the hood, frizzy wet curls flopping into her face. Trinity was already standing on the roof, peering down, a bottle in each hand. Her disintegrating updo looked regal above her big-shouldered coat.

Luddock muttered, "Oh, she's trashed. We're never getting home."

A flash of blond caught Clint's eye. Ursula crossing the icy lot, her heels tipping her heavy on the arm of the tuxedo man.

Clint flinched for Anna, but he still wanted her to turn and see. He wanted her to turn from where she was digging heel marks in the hood of Trinity's car, and see. Anna was watching Trinity slither off the trunk. If she just turned her head....

Trinity skittered out of the sodium glare of the light-pole, into the thick dark on the other side of the car, where the snowplows threw dirty snow and rocks and garbage. "Where's she...going...." said Luddock.

Ursula and her man were between Clint and Anna, oblivious to all the Tech drama. Ursula probably had powerlocks, keyless entry. She had everything, but if Clint called, "Hey,

Anna!" Anna would pivot and see blond and dark approaching a single car. Maybe she wouldn't care, maybe things were like that. Or maybe things were with Anna the way they were with Clint: when she saw the one she wanted wanting someone else, it would be a cold bolt sliding shut in the bottom of her stomach.

Clint didn't yell, or whistle, or even let Luddock follow his gaze. He just whispered to himself, Luddock, the world, "No." He looked at the car. Anna was alone now, yelling into the dark where Trinity must have stood. Anna was standing on the hood, laughing, snow on her hair.

He drank some more wine. Luddock's grip tightened on his shoulders. Something dark and heavy flew out of the parking-lot night, and smashed Trinity's car window.

DANIEL GRIFFIN

Mercedes Buyer's Guide

Wayne Krause claimed to know nothing about the stuff in the trunk of the car. The car had been his mother's and Wayne said he hadn't been up to sorting through it after the funeral. He did say that he was pretty sure the microwave worked. When it turned out it didn't and the toaster wouldn't keep bread down and both casserole dishes were cracked, Harry Stouffer suspected that Wayne had piled all that junk in just to get rid of it. Harry set the kitchenware, the typewriter, the bags of old shoes, the twelve windshield wiper blades and everything else in the corner of his garage. He vacuumed, sprayed air freshener into the car and tried to forget about Wayne Krause. Things kept turning up in that car though, things that kept Wayne and his family at the front of Harry's mind.

The first time Harry adjusted the passenger's seat he found a letter caught in the shifting mechanism. It was dated 12 January 1969. He spent some time wondering how a 1969 letter might have wound up in a 1981 car. Equally strange, the letter was written as if it were mid-summer. It complained of heat, drought and dust. Harry read it to himself three times before taking it inside where he asked his wife to guess what he'd just found in the car. "Another microwave," she said. Her books were fanned out before her. Harry knew she didn't want to be disturbed. The kids were asleep. This was her study time. He read it aloud anyway. Along with talk of weather there was mention of Myrna's health, a planned trip to the seaside and a cancelled New Years Eve party. "Isn't this neat?"

"Yeah," Colleen said. "Neat."

"I think it's from Australia." Harry re-folded the letter, tapped it against his palm. Colleen marked her spot in one book, turned to read from another. It was still a couple of weeks before exams, but she'd been working like this every night for a month.

"On the radio this morning they said you remember most if you study before sleep," Harry said. "Turns out whatever you were last thinking goes round and round in your brain all night." He waited for a response. Colleen looked up, nodded. "Neat, eh?" She nodded again.

Every night of his life Harry had had a shower before bed. Imagine how much smarter he'd be if he'd read the paper or the encyclopaedia. Of course the Stouffers didn't have an encyclopaedia. But still.

A week after finding the letter, Harry found thirty-two hundred dollars in a yellow envelope in the trunk. It was tucked under the lining, hidden or lost. He found it while returning the spare tire to its well. But that was a week later. Before finding the money, before Harry had even looked at the spare, he took the Australian letter over to Wayne Krause's place. It was after work on a Tuesday. Harry parked out front and walked across a yard full of toys—a trike, wagon, small slide, a couple of hoola-hoops. Wayne lived in a cul-de-sac in the Garrison development which meant his kids could leave things lying around like that. It also meant his kids could run around in the front yard without worry. If Harry's kids left something out after dark it would be gone by morning. And if they stepped off the sidewalk and into the street they'd be dead. A car would zip along and Bang. Harry didn't like to think about it. He didn't appreciate thoughts like this visiting him. It was true though. Zip, bang. Cars travelled way too fast on Bayshore. All the way down, greens fell in line. If Colleen wanted to become an engineer, Harry was fine with that. For starters she could re-engineer the traffic lights on Bayshore.

Harry looked at his watch as he rang the bell. He'd have to make it quick. He hadn't told Col that he was stopping at

Wayne's. He counted to ten, rang the bell again. Dum dee dum dee dum. A little girl opened the door. Harry crouched. "Hi kid, what's your name?"

"Lisa Krause." She was wearing a Barbie T-shirt.

"That's a sweet name," Harry said. "I'm Harry. Would you tell your dad that Harry's here?"

"Harry's here," she said, but she was still looking at Harry and hadn't raised her voice.

"Harry who?" Wayne yelled from somewhere inside.

"Harry Stouffer."

"Stouffer?"

"Like the frozen dinners." That brought no response. "Harry you sold the car to."

That did it. There was movement inside, then Wayne appeared, stomping down the hallway, feet, arms and belly all on the move. He looked like a boxer who'd been set loose on the world of doughnuts and fast food. "I don't know what's wrong with that car, but it was running when I sold it to you—"

"No, no, it's not about that—"

"—as is, remember. That's what we said." Harry held up his hands, shook his head and looked at his feet. "What?" Wayne said after a pause. "What?"

"You have any family in Australia? Any close family friends or anything?" Wayne filled the doorframe and the way he was looking at Harry right now made Harry worry about his size. A man that big could really inflict some pain. Harry's scalp warmed. "Anyone who lived in Australia in 1969?" Wayne kept looking at Harry in that peculiar way. Harry pulled out the letter. He said it had been under the passenger's seat.

Wayne stepped back into better light, read, flipped the letter over, read the reverse. "Helen," he said. The salutation was smudged but the letter had been clearly signed by Helen M. For a moment Wayne stood in silence then he turned.

"Hey, Mer," he yelled. "Get me the phone."

Lisa came out with it. Wayne dialled, stepped into the living-room and beckoned Harry. It occurred to Harry just then that he didn't really want an answer. He hadn't spent enough time daydreaming about the letter; he hadn't even shown it around work. All day it had sat in the glove compartment. And now that it was in Wayne's big fist, Harry was unlikely to get it back.

"Impulse," Harry said out loud. Wayne turned to look at him, but just then someone picked up on the other end and Wayne spoke into the phone. Col often said that Harry had to stop letting impulse carry him away.

Wayne covered the receiver. "Could it be South Africa? It could be, right?" Harry nodded. Of course it could. That hadn't occurred to Harry. "Helen," Wayne said into the phone. "Helen M." Harry must have assumed Australia because he and Tim had watched a documentary about dingos a couple of months ago, before the TV broke.

Wayne covered the phone again, yelled for someone to get him a map or an atlas or something. Eventually Lisa brought in a map of North America. Wayne un-folded it, turned it over. "Jesus weeps. A world map. A map with frigging Africa on it."

In the end they used a map on the inside cover of a dictionary. Wayne pointed to South Africa as if Harry might not have heard of it. "That's the spot. Right there." His finger covered half the country.

On the verandah, Wayne said he was sorry about all the junk in the car. He waved one of his big hands. "I just didn't want to deal with it. My mother's stuff and all. I get emotional about these things." Wayne pinched the bridge of his nose, closed his eyes and gave his head a shake. It wasn't easy watching someone as big as Wayne get emotional. Harry turned away to give the man some privacy. As he stood gazing down the street, he pictured the collection of wiper blades

61

that still sat in his garage. Who would even have a dozen wiper blades? The rest of the junk Harry sort of understood but a dozen wipers? The screen door banged and Wayne was back inside. He hadn't even said goodbye.

When Harry got home, Tim was playing tennis against the wall in the living-room and Sashi was bouncing on the sofa singing something from "The Lion King." Harry leaned in. "You'll break the springs, Sashi." Thwack. The ball hit the wall only inches from Harry's face. "Cut that out." It rolled under the stereo, and Harry headed down the hallway. Thwack. "Jesus weeps." Harry liked that curse. He thought he might start using it regularly. In the kitchen Colleen had her books out. Thwack. "Jesus weeps," Harry said again.
    "What's that?"
    "Why don't we just get a new TV? Something cheap."
    "It'll rot their minds."
    "It'll calm them down. They're tearing the house apart. Just go look at them."
    There was a thud that wasn't the tennis ball. Sashi came running into the kitchen and straight into Col's arms. From the living-room Tim shouted, "Wasn't me, wasn't me." Col rocked Sashi a while then returned one hand to working the calculator. Thwack.
    "Tim, do that somewhere else."
    "Where?"
    "Outside."
    "I'm grounded."
    "In the yard."
    "It's dark." The boy thumped down the hallway, poked his head into the kitchen. "What's for supper?" Oh shit. Harry had forgotten it was his turn to cook tonight. He opened his mouth to suggest they order pizza, but he already knew what Col would say. He turned to the cupboards. "Let me think a sec."

"You didn't stop at the grocery?"

"Thought I'd just make something from what we have here." Sashi was calm now, but she still leaned into her mother, enjoying the attention. Harry wouldn't have minded some attention. He wouldn't have minded leaning into Col and having her run her hand through his hair. Maybe he should jump up and down and fall off the chesterfield even after someone's told him not to. Thwack. "Tim, for Christ's sakes."

Eggs. He'd make eggs.

Harry diced an onion, grated some cheese, sliced a tomato and set a pan on the stove. He cracked eight eggs, buttered bread then asked Colleen if she could please clear away her books.

When everyone was at the table, Sashi raised her milk. "It's my turn tonight," she announced. "And I want to make a toast to the Queen."

Tim said, "Boring," but it was Sashi's turn so they all raised their glasses. Harry kept his thoughts about this exercise to himself. With the others he said, "To the Queen."

At 10.47 on Saturday, 25 April, Harry found thirty-two hundred dollars in the trunk of the car. The day before, he'd noticed that the rear tires didn't match and he'd wanted to check the spare, see if it was the missing mate. It wasn't and getting it back in proved a bugger. Harry ended up pulling the whole lining off. That's when he noticed the corner of the yellow envelope. Straight away he knew it was money. And straight away he knew that unless it was Canadian Tire money or something, he had his hands on a good chunk of change. He peeked in. Full of twenties. His legs went rubbery. He had to sit. He opened one of the lawn chairs, took a load off and began flipping through the wad. One hundred and sixty twenties made thirty-two hundred dollars. "Jesus weeps." He'd only paid nineteen hundred. And that was a deal. The car was nearly twenty years old and eaten by rust, but it was still a Mercedes.

Harry tapped the envelope against his thigh, money tight in his right hand. Thirty-two hundred dollars. Imagine the things you could do with thirty-two hundred dollars. Col would want to put it into savings or a mortgage payment or something. She might be okay spending some on the kids. Horse riding lessons for Sashi. Tennis lessons for Tim. Although Tim didn't really like tennis. He just liked banging the ball against the wall. He liked comic-books, but that would be a waste. What about a new television? The boy would love that. Everyone would. It could be a present for the whole family.

Colleen was on the back porch having her one cigarette of the day when Harry stepped out of the garage. At least, Harry hoped it was her one cigarette of the day. He didn't want to ask in case she got upset. It was only eleven. It was early to be having her one cigarette. You could bet she'd be needing another by six. She'd be desperate by nine. Harry considered saying something like that, making it a joke, only then Col turned and noticed him. Instead Harry said, "Guess what I found in the car."

"I don't know. What?"

"Colleen," he said. "Look at me."

"I am looking at you."

Harry threw the money in the air. It took Col a moment to understand what it was, and then she seemed to melt. Harry watched her carefully. More than anything he'd wanted to see Col's reaction. Her eyes grew big and milky. "Harry," she said. "Harry." Her knees went soft, bent a moment. Bills fluttered everywhere. It was like hitting big cash in a game show. The air was money.

"Three thousand two hundred dollars," Harry said. Col brought her hands to her mouth. She ran on the spot, jumped up and down, dropped her cigarette. By now the money was blowing all over the muddy yard. They noticed this at the same time. Some bills were already near the fence. Harry chased after them while Colleen bent to gather what was on the porch. "Kids," she yelled. "Hey kids!"

Harry ran along the fence line scooping up bills. When he looked back, Tim and Sashi were standing at the door. "Help pick up all this money before it blows away." For a moment the kids stood watching their parents scramble about then began chasing after bills themselves.

When they'd collected all of them, Colleen counted. 158. Two missing. Harry told Tim to hop into Mister Yee's yard, and Sashi crawled under the porch with a flashlight. After Tim found one of the missing bills they gave up. Harry felt a little bad about losing the other, but when he thought about Col's reaction, it had been worth twenty bucks. She'd melted. She really had.

Inside they had Cokes to celebrate. Colleen proposed a toast. "To thirty-two hundred dollars," she said. They tapped cans, drank. "To being rich," Tim said. They tapped cans again and Sashi said, "To being the richest." After the excitement had died a little, Harry called a family meeting. He'd never called one before. It had always been Col, but today he said they had to decide how to spend the dough.

"Har," Col said. "Har." She touched his shoulder. "Maybe we shouldn't talk about it like this. Maybe we should think about it a while, not do anything impulsive."

"We can discuss it though," Harry said. "No harm in talking, right? And I wasn't thinking we should spend it all, either. We should definitely put some aside for savings. More than some. A good chunk. Most of it. But I thought we could do something special with the rest. You've been complaining about having to take textbooks out of the library, so why not buy some? Sashi's been wanting riding lessons and Tim—"

"A TV," Tim said. He said it right on cue. It couldn't have been better if they'd planned it. Harry clapped his son on the back. "That's an idea." He couldn't remember when he'd been happier with something Tim had said. "A TV," the boy said again. It gave Harry a pinch of regret for having grounded him. He'd overreacted. He saw that now. The lamp had been old, worthless really.

"Maybe that could be the present to the whole family. The rest goes to savings or to the mortgage." Harry was trying to make it seem like he hadn't thought this through.

"Har." Col wasn't buying. She shook her head, but then Tim started chanting, "TV, TV." Sashi joined in and Harry couldn't help but grin. "Some textbooks too," he said, pointing at his wife.

"Everyone." Col raised her voice, but Tim and Sashi kept chanting and banging on the table. Harry took the money out, threw it in the air. It filled the room, rose to the lamp, fluttered ground-ward like dead leaves. Tim stood to bat at the bills. Sashi began running around the kitchen. Finally Colleen broke into a smile and started nodding. She scooped up some money, threw it in the air, scooped up more, threw it at Harry.

By 4.36 that afternoon they were all watching the new television. Lassie was on. Without cable there weren't many options. Harry couldn't find his glasses but the screen was big enough that he could do without. He was just thinking how he'd want them for the hockey tonight when it occurred to him that there might be more money in the car. Think of all the things they'd left in there. A microwave, a toaster, typewriter, shoes, an old letter and a wad of cash. Obviously not very careful people. Obviously not very well organized. Not that Harry was either of these things, and not that he was complaining, but still.

"What if there's more money in there?" Harry said during the next commercial. "What if they were really rich and just had lots of cash lying here there and everywhere? They had a

66

Mercedes after all. Plus at least thirty-two hundred in cash."

"We have a Mercedes and thirty-two hundred in cash," Tim said.

Harry patted him on the knee. "You're right there son." And then Harry stood. "Who wants to help me search the car?" No-one answered. Harry said, "Who wants more money?" and Tim's ears perked up. "If I find more money, who do you think should keep it?"

Tim stood. "Whoever wants some money had better come help." Good old Tim. It was nice to be getting along so well. They'd had a lot of fights recently, and that whole incident with Grandmother's lamp had cast a long shadow.

In the end they all went. Colleen put on rubber gloves, groped between the seats. She found some tissue, a pen, a pair of broken sunglasses and an unsigned birthday card for a 95-year-old.

Tim searched the doors—their pockets, handles, trim panels, armrests and ashtrays. Harry gave Sashi the flashlight and coerced her into searching the trunk. He told everyone to keep an eye out for his glasses then began removing the front seats. He knew this was taking things a bit far, but he wanted to be thorough. By the time he had the second one out, Col and Sashi had gone back inside. Tim was just watching. There was nothing of interest under either seat. Tim tried sitting in one. The springs gave an old man's sigh.

Harry crouched where the passenger seat had been, emptied the glove compartment. Stuck in a crevice was a driver's licence for Barbara Krause. She was pictured in the corner looking startled and pale. It had expired in 1988. Harry held it up to show Tim, but his son had left too.

Harry removed the dashboard cover. Underneath, he poked about the instrument panel's wiring, the heater unit, the passages that led to the vents. He began on the steering-column then realized it was six o'clock. It was also a Saturday which meant it was his turn to cook. He walked in whis-

67

pering, "Pizza, pizza, pizza." Tim and Sashi screamed their approval but minutes later bickered over the toppings as they always did.

While tipping the deliveryman, Harry realized that the money hadn't been lost or misplaced. No-one would misplace thirty-two hundred dollars. They'd hid it deliberately. Old people always hid money. They distrusted banks. And if the Krauses had hidden more, wouldn't it be somewhere unusual? He'd have to search the entire car. Every inch.

Harry didn't watch "Hockey Night in Canada." Instead he removed the roof panelling, pulled up the carpeting and took the trim off the doors. He checked the rusty bumpers, the rusty wheel wells, looked over the whole rusty underbody. He removed one piece of the side moulding just to assure himself nothing could fit in it. He didn't give up until five past eleven by which time half the car seemed to be strewn about the garage. Harry hadn't found a penny. He hadn't even found his glasses.

On 16 September, 1980 a silver Mercedes 126-S rolled off the S-Class line at the Daimler-Benz plant in Sindelfingen, West Germany. It was near the end of the second shift. The red light had been on all day indicating the assembly line was behind quota. What was more, it was Torsten Fast's birthday and his family would soon be gathered and waiting for him. All the same, Torsten took his time on this last car, examined its heating and air conditioning systems, its instrument cluster and steering-column then noticed a piece of paper lying on the floor. He bent, lifted it. *"Gutten geburtztag Schatz."* Torsten looked about, smiled self-consciously, tucked the note into his pocket and turned fully around. No-one was watching. He patted the car and moved on. Torsten gave every car he inspected a tap on the hood. He called it his *letzter kuss.*

The car left the plant by train bound for the port of

Bremerhaven and travelled to Montreal by containership where it cleared customs and was inspected, tagged and transferred to an eighteen-wheeler at the Mercedes preparation centre. While driving it onto the trailer, Martin Roche brushed it against a concrete pillar. He'd been adjusting the radio so he could listen to something for the few seconds it took to move the car. The contact left a small scrape and a shallow dent, but Roche was the only person to notice. His palms grew damp and his stomach did somersaults until after the driver had signed for the cars and was headed for Markham. The moment the truck was out of the prep centre that scrape could have happened anywhere. Roche swore up and down that he'd be more careful. He'd only had the job two weeks and at this rate he wouldn't last long.

The silver 126-S arrived along with two C-class sedans and a station-wagon at the Frank Cherry dealership next morning and Frank had a fit. He spotted the scrape straight off. He had an eye for that sort of thing. He said he'd send it back, said he'd send the whole load right back to fucking Germany. His son-in-law told him they could fix it, but Frank wasn't listening. He gripped his chest. Was someone trying to kill him? Didn't they know he had a heart condition? Frank was at the loading entrance, but customers could still hear. Barbara Krause blushed. The man had to be 70 and here he was carrying on like a twelve-year-old. She tried not to listen. On the way back into the showroom Frank Cherry said he wanted someone fired for this. His face was bright red. Cherry, Barbara thought.

Tuesday evening Harry remembered to stop at the grocery store. He picked up sausages, potatoes and a head of cabbage. The Garrison development was only a couple K away and Harry found himself turning toward Wayne's place. All the toys were still strewn across the front lawn. It had been a week but they seemed to be in exactly the same spots.

Lisa answered the door. Harry crouched. "Would you tell your dad that Harry's here?"

"Harry who?" Wayne called.

"Stouffer. Like the frozen dinners." Wayne stepped into the hall, wiped his mouth with a serviette. "I'm sorry." Harry stood. "Hope I'm not interrupting anything. Not eating are you?"

"No, no, come on in. Find any more letters?" Wayne chuckled. "My sister and I got a real kick out of that." The screen door banged behind Harry.

"I was just driving by and thought I'd. I just wanted to know. I could have called for this but I lost your number. Hi Lisa." Harry was having trouble getting to his question. He was no longer even sure what his question was. He wanted to know something. He wanted to know a lot of things. Things about the elderly parents who'd hidden money in their car, the great aunt living in South Africa, the startled face staring out of the driver's licence, the birthday card for a 95-year-old, the windshield wiper blades and all the other junk in the car. He wanted to know about all of these things, but he didn't know how to begin. Wayne was still staring at him. Lisa was staring at him. Neither ever seemed to blink. Harry dug both hands into his jacket pockets, felt the taped arm of his second pair of specs. He shifted from foot to foot. How do you ask? Where do you start?

"Harry?" Wayne said, and Harry took a deep breath. "Something wrong, Harry?"

"I can't find my glasses. I didn't leave my glasses here did I?"

"He leave his glasses here?" Wayne called over his shoulder.

"No."

Harry nodded. He nodded as hard as he could and said he wouldn't bother them again. He waved to Lisa and waited for her to wave back. She didn't.

Ken Krause liked the idea of a scraped car. He liked the idea of saving a grand for a scrape and a dent which they could fix and make imperceptible. Plus there'd be no waiting list. It could be his today. Barbara wasn't so sure. Wouldn't it decrease the resale value? Wouldn't it rust? And didn't it seem strange to spend $30,000 for a damaged car? She didn't say all of this, at least not in so few words. She said she didn't like silver. Too flashy, too much glitter. And she spent a long time standing near the one she did like. It was deep green and in perfect condition. Eventually she pulled Ken aside and asked if they shouldn't at least look at some others.

"Lovey, I'm negotiating. Just let me take care of this. Please." But Barbara could see that the only thing Ken was taking care of was that silver car. They'd be stuck with it. She knew it.

In the lounge Barbara lit a cigarette. She shouldn't be upset. It was a brand new car except for the scrape. But it bothered her all the same. For one thing, Jeannie would notice no matter how they painted it. Remember last year when she spotted that mark on Eloise's gown? It was tiny and they'd all but removed it, but in the end Eloise was in tears, blaming Barbara for spilling the mascara and ruining her wedding.

When Barbara returned to the showroom, Ken had the silver car on the street ready for a test drive. The two of them circled the nearby blocks, drove the highway a mile in each direction. Ken said it was an Arabian thoroughbred on wheels. Barbara said as little as possible. They parked in the lot. Ken went in for the paperwork. He asked if she wanted to join him. Barbara shook her head, lit a cigarette, switched on the radio. Ken was almost an hour in there and when he came out he had a toothy, owner's grin. He raised the keys, suddenly a little boy holding the best present ever. It lit her heart a moment. At the car he offered her the keys. "Do the honours?" but Barbara shook her head.

Ken pulled out of the lot, made a right onto Drummond Road. Barbara put a hand on his leg, let it lie there. She wanted to ask when they were going to fix the dent, but held back. Two blocks from the highway a snowball hit the windshield. A second hit the hood with a deep thud. Ken slammed his foot on the brakes, brought the car to an abrupt halt. Barbara wasn't wearing her seatbelt. Her body hit the dash, her face hit the windscreen. Straining against his own belt, Ken lost his breath. His heart sputtered, clamoured against his rib cage. When the momentum was spent, Ken fell back against the seat and Barbara fell from the dash. She lifted a hand, groped at the armrest and pulled herself up. "You all right?" Ken said in a whisper.

"Yes. I think." She didn't say anything else. She ran fingers across her body, brought them to her face and sat slumped in the passenger seat.

"Goddam kids. Jesus." Ken unbuckled, climbed out of the car. He brought a hand to his chest. That had scared him. It really had. His knees trembled. All through his body he could feel it. Jesus what a scare.

No-one in sight. That was always the way. As soon as he drove away the little fuckers would be back. A car passed, horn blaring. Ken got back in, pulled over to the curb. Barbara lit a cigarette. "Give me one of those, will you?" Ken said. Barbara nodded, passed him hers and lit another. "Jesus." Ken banged a hand against the steering-wheel and that too hurt.

When Harry got home that night the TV was on. Tim and Sashi were quiet in front of it, faces illuminated by the flashing screen. Down the hall Col was studying at the kitchen table. Harry set the grocery bag on the counter and said he was making bangers and mash. He put a pot on the stove, peeled the potatoes, cut them in half so they'd cook more quickly, then sliced the cabbage, tossed it in the frying pan with the sausage.

Barbara Krause's driver's licence lay on the counter. Harry lifted it as the kids came down the hall for supper. For a moment, the sound of Col laying the cutlery evaporated and in that moment, Harry glimpsed beyond Barbara's startled face and into a sorrow that lay beneath. For an instant it could have been his own face in that licence, his wife's, even one of his kids'. It made Harry want to go back into the garage and sift through all those things that had cluttered the car, look for something he might have missed, not money, something more personal, something that would testify for Barbara: evidence she'd been here, engaged, participating.

When Harry turned, Col and the kids were seated and waiting. He set down the licence, walked to the table and raised his glass. "To life," he said. For a moment his children and his wife just looked at him. In all the weeks they'd been making toasts, Harry had never offered one, but now he held steady with his glass in the air until one by one, the family raised their cups and toasted life. They drank and when Harry sat, the family began to eat.

Promise

I slowed the car as we turned onto my brother's street. In the back, Tracy had her hand out the window. "Is it that one?" she said. "Or that one, or that one?"

The houses were similar enough that I wasn't sure myself until I spotted Marshall's *Gone Fishing* sign. His drive was empty, the curtains were closed, and it was almost noon on a Saturday. It occurred to me briefly that he might actually be fishing.

Tracy had been asking questions about Uncle Marshall the whole way up, but now she didn't want to get out of the car. I had to carry her up the lane on my hip.

Marshall's *Gone Fishing* sign hung above a constellation of rust spots at the centre of his door. I reached out to touch it just as the door opened. My brother filled the space, rubbed his eyes, then closed the door to remove the chain. "Well, well," he said. "Long time no see."

"Just dropping in for a quick visit." I tried to pry Tracy from my shoulder so she could say hello, but she tightened her grip, dug her face into me.

Marshall made space and we followed him down the carpeted hall and into the living-room where he collapsed into the corner of the sofa. "Make yourselves at home." Near his feet, the parts of a handgun were spread across a white towel—springs, levers, handle, barrel. Mother had told me about the gun.

"Sorry to barge in, just you know." I shrugged and filled my lungs while the disassembled pistol held my gaze. "Heard about Susan," I said at last.

"Figured that was why you were here."

"Mom's worried."

Marshall nodded a moment.

I crouched and faced Tracy. "Honey, you want to watch

74

TV?"

"Susan took the TV, which makes her a fucking thief, but you probably don't want to hear that."

"We could get some toys, some books or a Barbie? Lets see your backpack."

Tracy held it out. My daughter has two sets of everything—one for her mother's place, one for mine. These were toys from her mother's and less familiar to me. I unzipped the backpack as I led her through to the dining-room.

"After we're going to the park, right?" she said.

"Absolutely."

Marshall's dining-room table was littered with shopping bags, food wrappers and a few dirty plates. A small pile of unopened mail sat at one corner. When we were kids, Marshall and I had called the dining-room "the dying room." As I crossed back through the kitchen, I said to him, "Looks like you're doing all your living in the dying room." He didn't respond though. His expression didn't even change.

"She called me in hysterics," I said after a while.

"Who?"

"Mom. She mentioned a restraining order, assault charges. You getting a gun, which is obviously true."

"There's no assault charges, Doug."

"Okay," I said. "But—"

"It's just Dad's Luger. Was getting rusty in Mom's basement so I'm cleaning it up."

"She's worried is all."

"So why didn't she come up and say this?"

I shrugged. I hadn't asked her, but it did occur to me that she was a little afraid of Marshall. She might have also believed Marshall and I were closer than we were, that I might have access to some part of him denied to her.

I said none of this, and eventually Marshall said, "She'd rather have her errand boy do it."

"She probably thinks I can talk to you in a way she can't."

75

That made Marshall chuckle. He shifted, licked his lips. "And so what exactly are you supposed to be talking about?"

"Guess I'm just supposed to make sure you're okay, that you'll get through this. I mean—"

"So tell her."

"Okay," I said. "I'll tell her." My words trailed away, and the room seemed suddenly big, empty and quiet. Outside a crow swooped past, landed on the grass.

After high school, when Marshall and I began to veer apart, I'd started telling people that one of us had to have been adopted. Our trajectories continued to widen—he spent some time in the military, some time on probation, some time unemployed. I went to university, got a job, spent some time in the suburbs, some time at the Ministry of Transportation, some time in divorce court. Nowadays we saw each other for Christmas and most years that was it.

"Moment you came in, I figured you were here to kick me when I'm down," Marshall said.

"I get two weekends a month with Tracy so I'm not about to waste one—"

"It's a power trip, Doug. That's all this is. Susan's fucking with me. Restraining orders are meaningless. I could get a restraining order against Mr. Johansson for letting his dog shit on my lawn. Plus her mother made her get it." Marshall pursed his lips, scratched the tip of his nose. "We're working it out, actually. Couple therapy and that."

"You're going to couple therapy?"

"Can't be any worse than talking to you."

"Okay."

"Doug, did you ever have a sense of humour?"

"And you can go to couple therapy despite the restraining order? Legally speaking, I mean."

"I was just over there last night."

"Over where?"

"Susan's mother's place. Where she's staying."

"What about the restraining order?"

He lurched toward me then, half launched himself off the sofa. I was a few feet away, but still flinched. Marshall gave a shallow, breathy chuckle. "You don't fucking listen is your problem."

I wanted to smile, but my face didn't co-operate. My right eye started twitching. Tracy came trotting through the kitchen and into the living-room. "Time's up," she said. "It's time to go to Old McDonalds."

"Okay, honey, hold on a sec." I turned back to Marshall, took a deep breath. "We should probably go, but I'm glad you two are going to work it out. Mom will be happy to hear all this. I'm sure it's what she wanted."

Tracy gave my arm a pull. "Old McDonalds."

"Never met a woman who knew what she wanted," Marshall said.

I was ready to stand and go, but Marshall sat still, hunched in the corner of the sofa. Tracy pulled my sleeve again. "I thought we were going to the park, honey."

"Park then Old McDonalds."

"Old Macdonald had a farm," Marshall sang. Tracy turned toward him. Marshall sang on and a smile slowly rose to Tracy's face.

"That's not it," she said. "I'm talking about the Old McDonalds you eat at."

"That's just McDonalds. It's called McDonalds. Old Macdonald had a farm, Ronald McDonald had a hamburger."

"You're silly."

"Worse than silly. I'm stupid."

Tracy set a hand on my knee. "Stupid's a bad word." Her voice was just above a whisper.

"Listen, we should probably get going and leave you to it." I stood. "Next time you're down our way you should come by."

"There's a park down the road." Marshall gestured toward

the street. "Swings and all that."

"Go get your things, honey. I'll be right with you, okay?"

We both watched Tracy cross through the kitchen. "She's kind of duck footed, isn't she?" Marshall said. Before I could respond, a siren sounded in the distance. We both turned, cocked our heads. Tracy came running in and pressed herself against me, covered her ears. Moments later the fire engine passed right in front of the house. The siren began to fade then slowed and stopped all together.

Marshall walked to the door. "Maybe the whole neighbourhood will burn, and I can get some insurance money."

I turned to Tracy. "Lets get your things picked up."

Marshall was gone by the time we returned to the front door. We stepped outside. He was half-way down the block, walking toward the billows of dark smoke with a stoop that hid his height. Two fire engines parked in the middle of the road had their hoses trained on the fire. Water had already reached the gutter in front of Marshall's place. "Come on, let's go say goodbye."

Tracy raised her arms and when I lifted her, she held on tight.

I'd intended to simply say goodbye, but we didn't reach Marshall until he was at the edge of a small crowd. He turned as we neared. "It's about time someone cleaned that place out. Fucking crack house. Whole area is going to shit."

A red headed woman looked over. The heavy-set man next to her also turned. "You mind?" he said.

"It's a crack house."

The man stepped closer, pushed Marshall back. My brother stumbled but recovered. He raised his fists, took a couple of swings before a tall man grabbed him and held on. Tracy screamed and I instinctively backed away. "Just fuck off," a woman yelled.

I began walking back to the car, both arms tight around Tracy while she wailed in my ear. "It's okay, honey," I said.

"Everything's fine. We're all okay."

By the time Marshall caught up, I had Tracy buckled into the car seat.

"No park then, huh?" Marshall's shirt was torn open, but otherwise he looked unhurt.

"Call if you need anything," I said.

"Doug, you are such a fucking shit."

"What?"

"I haven't seen you in what, six months, and you come up here and expect me to get on my knees or something."

"I'll tell Mom not to worry."

"You're just like her. You should have been born a woman."

I slid into the driver's seat.

"All our lives you managed to slip in and out, duck the worst of it while it lands on me. It really is amazing."

I started the engine, pulled out of the drive. I waved without looking at him. Behind me, Tracy sniffled. She wiped her nose. At the first corner, she said, "Don't forget Old McDonalds."

"Will you quit bugging me about Old McDonalds?"

For a while after that, the only sound was the engine and the thumping of my heart. I adjusted the rearview mirror. Tracy was gazing out her window. "Why were they fighting?"

"I don't know, honey. Uncle Marshall gets himself in trouble sometimes."

"Is he still in trouble?"

"Don't know. Hope not."

Near the highway, I pulled over for gas. While the cashier charged my credit card, I flipped through a phone book that lay on the counter. It listed Susan's mother's address on Helmken Street. I asked for directions. Back in the car, I told Tracy we had one more stop. "On the way to Old McDonalds."

"Quick, okay?"

Helmken borders forest. Deep dark stands of cedar climb a gentle slope on one side of the street. In this part of the island, people live on the cleaned-up corners of the land. Wilderness begins at the end of every street. Two steps off the paved road the world turns raw and wild.

I pulled over at number 218. "Sit tight," I said. "Be right back."

The sun was high now and free of clouds. It warmed the crown of my head as I knocked. The door opened slowly, still chained. "Susan?" I said. "It's—"

"He ask you to come?"

"I was just talking to him and. I mean. Are you two still seeing each other?" Susan leaned forward, peering toward the car. The movement revealed the rest of her face. Purple feathered out from a dark ring under her right eye.

"Jesus," I said.

She watched me in silence.

"He talked about." I took a long, deep breath. "About maybe working things out, getting back together."

Susan shook her head and closed the door. Half of me expected her to unchain and fully open it, but instead the lock slid into place.

"I'm sorry," I called.

"He sets foot anywhere near me and I'm calling the police. Tell him that."

Tracy ate. I had no appetite. I drank coffee, watched while she ran around the Playplace.

One summer when Marshall and I were kids, we biked out to McDonalds almost every day. We took the money from our father's wallet. Eventually he caught Marshall with the wallet open. Dad caned him so badly that from where I was hiding in the attic, I could still hear Marshall scream. I was huddled under the rafters, head pressed against a beam so hard that a splinter cut into my cheek.

That was the summer Marshall and I formed a gang. It was just the two of us, but we had rules, daily meetings, oaths of loyalty. The attic was our headquarters and it was up there that Marshall and I pricked our fingers and held them together, let the blood mingle.

When Tracy was done playing, I drove us back to Marshall's. The fire trucks were still in view, but the crowd had disappeared, and the smoke had slowed to a trickle. Tracy stared at the trucks in silence. I shifted in my seat, watched her a moment. "One hot minute," I said.

Tracy didn't look at me. The fire trucks held her. "If my house burned down, I'd come and live with you," she said.

"That's right."

"Could Mom come too?"

"Of course."

I waited for her to say something more, but she didn't. She simply gazed out the window.

I knocked on Marshall's door until he answered. "You again," he said.

"Sorry about how things ended."

"Doug, you are such a pussy."

"After McDonald's we were about to head home only I wanted to come by and say that. Mind if I use your washroom before we get back on the road?"

Marshall made space. I stepped inside.

"Keep an eye on Tracy for me? She's still in the car." At the bathroom door, I turned and watched Marshall step onto the porch. Once he was out, I ducked into the living-room, crouched before the disassembled pistol. I took the most important looking piece I could find. It was the hammer, the ignition system. It's wide and flat. Like an iceberg, the larger part hangs out of sight.

From the moment I left Marshall's house, I was expecting an angry phone call. I had images of him coming after me, but in the days that followed, Marshall never mentioned the hammer. He may not have even realized it was missing. As far as I know, he never tried to reassemble the Luger. And in the end it didn't matter. In the end, he used a knife.

"X"

A raccoon mauled my mother's cat so badly it took $300 to stitch him up. The next afternoon, she called to ask if I could help her get rid of the animal. "The vet went on and on about rabies," she said. "What if it bit me? When they get rabies, they go a little batty."

I told her I didn't know how to catch a raccoon. On the sofa across from me, my roommate Alfie raised his arms like he was firing a rifle. "Boom," he said. "Take it out in one shot."

"You rent traps," Mom said. "They come with instructions. All you need is bait."

"When would you want this?"

"Maybe this weekend?"

Her urgency should have told me something more was going on, but at the time I thought nothing of it and said I'd be up Friday evening.

After I hung up, Alfie pushed the bong my way. "Ryan, you can set out traps all month, or take a rifle and be done with it." While I took a hit, he walked into his bedroom, brought back the Lee-Enfield his grandfather had given him. He set it in my hands. "This sucker will blow a raccoon into next week."

I spent a moment getting a feel for the rifle, ran my hand down the fine grain of the stock and along the icy barrel, etched and pock-marked by time. Just touching it sent a shiver of electric cold right through my thick dopey haze. Imagine the damage this thing must have done in its lifetime. I raised it to look down the sight line.

"Jesus," Alfie said, "Don't be pointing that at me." He lit the bong, took a hit and batted the smoke away while I laid the rifle across my lap. "Don't even joke about that shit."

After Orillia, traffic was light. Islands of muddied snow appeared on the side of the road. By the time I reached the cottage, the late afternoon sun was sparkling off hardened roadside snowbanks that would lie on the ground for weeks to come.

Mom stepped out to greet me. "You made it," she said as if it had been in doubt. We hugged and she led me up the flagstone path and inside. "You must be tired. All that driving." She squeezed my shoulders, guided me to a chair at the kitchen table.

The cottage had been in my father's family for years, but during the divorce it wound up in my mother's hands. Over the past two years, she'd rebuilt it, winterized, modernized. The doorway where I'd tripped and broken my arm was gone along with the wall that had divided kitchen and living-room. She'd doubled the size of the deck. The kitchen was all new, including the island where she now stood chopping parsley. Her knife built up a steady rhythm. "Now, you must tell me about Sandra," she said.

I tried to read her expression, but her head was down, eyes on her work. "Okay. What do you want to know?"

She looked up, but didn't speak, just lifted a dishtowel and wiped her hands. She seemed to be struggling for words and that put a knot in my throat. Sandy must have told her she was pregnant. Or maybe Sandy's mother told her. Someone. But all I said was, "I don't really see her much since we broke up," and then I glanced back out the big bay windows toward the lake, glassy calm, just the tiniest ripples at its centre.

"Right," Mom said. "Of course."

On the far side of the lake, the last of the day's sunlight reflected off the windows of cottages forming a ragged trail of glinting lights.

"Oh, look at me." Her voice was now high and tight. "I haven't even offered a drink. Wine or beer? I have both."

"Beer." My finger traced a line in the table's dark grain. "Brought a rifle," I said.

"A what?"

"For the raccoons."

"Of course." She forced a chuckle. "The raccoons." She opened a bottle of beer. I stood, walked over to accept it. "Bought the ones you like. With the picture of sailboats." She returned to the fridge for the wine.

"Have you been talking to Sandy?" I said while her back was turned.

"Let me get supper on the table. I shouldn't have started asking about Sandra. I don't know where my mind is." She moved from the fridge to the stove without looking my way. She stirred a pot, tasted something from the fry pan. My mother's thinner than she should be. A wiry woman, she moves with a frantic energy. She bustles, especially in the kitchen.

"The reason I ask—" I said.

"Now hold on a moment, honey." At the sink, she emptied the pot into a colander. Steam rose in a column and mushroomed above her head. She set the pot aside and turned. She folded her arms, showed her teeth as if forcing a smile. "Truth is last weekend Sandra phoned to invite me to the shower. She thought I knew. At first I didn't understand. I thought maybe this was some strange way of telling me you were back together and getting married. I guess this was just the last thing I expected."

"I'm sorry," I said, although it probably wasn't audible. "I know what you must be thinking. I've been wanting to. Meaning to."

"I'm not thinking anything." She tossed the dishtowel onto the counter. "I'm just glad it's out. I feel relieved." She bowed her head, ran a finger under one eye. "I promised myself I wouldn't cry and now look at me."

My mother stepped forward, set her hands on my shoulders, held me at arms length a moment. A tear formed. I blinked it away, sniffled and she pulled me close. Big inevitable tears were on their way, though what I wanted just then, more than anything, was not to be making such a fucking big deal of this. I bit down on my lip, wiped away another tear.

"Honey, I know it must be hard, but this is also wonderful news. One day you'll see that." She dug her fingers into my back, held on tight for a moment.

There were a lot of reasons I hadn't told her about the preg- nancy. For a time I wondered if the baby was even mine. Sandy and I were together only once last fall. We bumped into each other at a party. We were drunk. Returning to the apartment we'd once shared was easy and comfortable, though I didn't even stay the night. After she found out, we talked about getting back together, but neither of us really wanted to. I tried to convince her to get an abortion. For the past two months I hadn't seen Sandy at all. I was either working or holed up with Alfie, smoking dope and avoiding life.

"You don't need to feel ashamed."

"I'm not ashamed. I just. I was planning to tell you this weekend."

"I shouldn't have opened my big mouth. I promised myself I'd give you the weekend to tell me. Or however long you stay. I mean, I was only going to raise the topic when you were leaving." She pulled away. She was trying to smile. "I'd rehearsed being surprised and everything." She threw up her hands, gave her best surprised look.

The Lee-Enfield is a bolt-action rifle. It fires a .303 cartridge from a five-round detachable clip. 44 $\frac{1}{2}$ inches long, it weighs eight pounds ten ounces unloaded. It has a muzzle velocity of 2440 feet per second and an effective range of 1200 yards. It was used by British and Commonwealth forces during both world wars and is still used by the Reserve forces in Canada. The rifle also remains popular with hunters.

After supper, I put a trap at either end of the fence the raccoons often scrambled along. I set a can of tuna in the back of
each, then propped open the door. The moon had ducked
behind clouds and on my way to collect the rifle, I tripped
over the woodpile.

Holding the Lee-Enfield in the cold, I practised raising it,
drew a bead on one of my mother's trees, squeezed the trigger.
The mechanism clicked. I drew a bead on the half obscured
moon then lowered the rifle to the streaks of light across the
dark water, pulled the trigger again. "Bang," I said.

I left the rifle in the enclosed porch. My mother didn't look
up as I stashed the bullets in the cabinet, rubbed my hands
together to regain some warmth. The fire had crumbled into
a pile of red coals. Mom was sitting close to it, knitting.
"Have you told your sister?" she said.

I nodded, flopped into the armchair and pulled the dish of
nuts closer.

"Oh, darling, does everyone know but me?"

"I see her every couple of weeks, Mom. It just came out."

"We talk on the phone every week."

"Don't take it personally. There's lots who don't know. I'm
going to have to send out a card or something. 'Newsflash:
Ryan knocks up ex-girlfriend'."

"Oh, Ryan, for goodness sakes."

I picked out a few cashews. "What are you knitting?"

"Supposed to be a sweater, but God only knows. It's a dis-
aster. How can a 50-year-old learn to knit?" She held it up, a
short green flap of material dangled from two needles. "This
little kid is just going to melt your heart, Ryan, I swear."

My mother's needles clicked away. I collected the rest of the
cashews in my hand, shook them like dice, popped a couple
into my mouth. Just months ago, when I was still pestering
Sandy to get an abortion, I'd said it was the only choice. We
were too young. Neither of us wanted to get back together.
She finally told me never to talk to her about it again. How do

you go from there to having the baby melt your heart?

"You're going to be a great dad," my mother said. "Once you get going."

"I got a letter calculating my child support payments. They start on 27 June. One hundred dollars a week beginning a month after Baby Severin's born."

Her needles stopped. She pulled down her glasses, looked at me above the rims. "The baby won't have your name?"

I shook my head. She pushed her glasses back up and tried to find her place in the knitting. "Maybe you'll get back together?"

"She's got a new boyfriend."

This time Mom set her knitting down completely. She looked at me, but no words came out.

"They've started living together. The kid will probably be calling him 'Dad'."

"Oh, Ryan, it doesn't have to be that way."

I shrugged. "Not sure I'm wanted."

"Have you given any indication that you want to be involved, like taking an interest in the pregnancy, meeting with the doctors, going to the hospital for the birth? Fathers are now expected in the delivery-room. Have you considered that?"

I didn't answer. I mean, what exactly is an unwanted, bio-logical father supposed to do during the birth?

"You know, your father didn't come to Lucy's, but he was there for yours. Times had changed by then and men were allowed in." She pointed her glasses toward me. "It was one of the most important experiences of his life."

"He never told me that."

"Well he told me."

"Alfie bought me a box of cigars."

My mother poked one arm of her glasses between her lips. "Alfie's a good kid."

I reclined the easy chair, switched on the TV. The cat

hopped onto my lap, began to purr. His thick marmalade fur was shaved where the vet had stitched his wounds. One of his ears was split almost the whole way down.

"I'm going to come," Mom said. "The moment I hear, I'm on my way."

"Great, that way if Sandy wants to scream at someone in the delivery-room, you can stand in for me."

"She might not want me in the delivery-room, but I'll come as close as I can get."

Raccoons range from 20 to 40 inches long and weigh up to 35 pounds. They are intelligent animals with a well-deserved reputation for mischievousness—their thumbs enable them to open garbage cans and doors. They carry approximately 50% of the documented animal rabies cases in North America. Last year, Toronto police recorded three instances of residents shooting raccoons within city limits.

My alarm sounded at quarter to six. I switched it off and rolled over. When my eyes opened again, the sun was creeping into the sky. I dressed, tiptoed into the hall, loaded the clip and stepped outside. Breath formed clouds in front of my face and my cheeks soon tingled from the cold. I leaned against my car, gazed out toward the road while light spread across the land.

There was no sign of any raccoons and soon the cold had a grip on me. I curled my toes in my boots and shuffled about trying to keep warm. Once the sun was well over the treeline on the other side of the lake, I lay down the rifle.

At my mother's woodpile, I picked up her axe, set a log on the chopping block. I tested the weight of the axe then swung. The top of the handle hit the wood and sent shock waves back to my hands. On the next swing, I embedded the blade, lifted log and axe wholesale and split it in two strikes. I set up another and kept chopping, slowly regaining confidence with the axe.

I chopped wood until I was winded. Blisters were forming on my hands and a warm ache radiated along my arms. I was on the high side of the lot and could see clear across the lake. The wind formed patterns, broad strokes across the water. Trail-like clouds lay in furrows over the trees. I leaned a hip against the axe, slowly caught my breath, enjoying the chilly breeze on my damp forehead.

I set up another log, swung the axe, split it, slowly worked myself back into a sweat. Once out of breath, I headed for the water. At the end of the lane, I started to run, took off my jacket, sweater, shirt. I arrived at the water stripped to the waist, dropped my pants and pulled off my boots. The water's ripples distorted my reflection. Standing on the diving rock, goose bumps rose along my arms and chest and I was suddenly shivering. When we were kids, before the divorce, we were up here every summer weekend. Our days centred around swimming and eating. Five or six times a day my sister and I would dive from this rock. At the time I knew every crack, every sharp corner and smooth edge. All that knowledge was gone, but the rock was still there, below me now, unchanged.

I crouched and dove, hit the water curled almost into a ball. My heart stopped a moment, seized by the cold of the lake, then it began to thunder, knocking against my ribs in quick, heavy blasts. I surfaced, chest so tight I could only pant. Teeth chattering, body quivering, I managed to turn, paddle, scramble up the rock. I scraped my knee, stubbed my toe, then was out of the water, reborn in the cold morning air.

I tried to pull on my jeans, but it was difficult with wet legs. My fingers were numb and dulled, my entire body in a frigid panic. I wrapped my arms around myself, ran with boots unlaced and collected my shirt, sweater and jacket on the way up the hill.

The third trimester of pregnancy begins at 28 weeks, which is the first week at which a preterm foetus is considered viable. By 32 weeks, the baby starts to get ready for birth, building fat and turning its head down. At this stage, the baby is about ten inches long and weighs more than a pound. Skin still translucent, the baby's lips, eyebrows, and eyelids are now distinct, and the baby's bones are beginning to harden.

After buying groceries, Mom drove us to a baby store outside Drysdale. We were the only shoppers until a young couple came in. They stood by us while my mother picked out pyjamas. "They're just so tiny," the woman said. "Look how cute."

"Shopping for my first grandchild."

The woman looked from my mother to me. I stood there, waiting for the conversation to tumble into humiliating territory—about my age, about not being married, about an unplanned pregnancy. But all she said was, "Congratulations. When's the baby due?"

"May 31st."

She put a hand across the top of her belly. "We're May 30th. Isn't that funny?"

The woman's husband pulled her away to look at strollers, and I said, "Why does everything for a baby need a different name? Onesie, sleeper, booties. Why not T-shirt, pyjamas and shoes?"

"Ryan, don't be such a grump. You sound like your father."

She rifled through another bin of clothes then lifted a book from a display on the shelf. "Looks like the one for you. Get you squared away with your fatherly duties."

I nodded, shrugged. Sandra was due in eight weeks yet my mother was the only person I could recall mentioning fatherly duties. When I asked Sandy what she wanted of me, she'd said, "Nothing. I mean, let's be realistic." Of course, she didn't really mean that because two months later I got the assessment of child support, which left me facing a Kraft Dinner diet for the next eighteen years. That was the fatherly duty weighing on my mind.

On the way out of the baby store, Mom said, "These clothes are for when you keep the baby. Okay?"

"What's the baby going to do in a two-bedroom apartment with Alfie and me?"

"Alfie can help out. It'll be good for him."

"Alfie smokes dope every morning before going to work at a gas station where he sells contraband cigarettes."

"Alfred? Our Alfred?"

"Don't look so surprised."

We climbed into her car and after a few moments of silence, she said, "Perhaps it's time you had your own apartment?"

"Mom," I said.

"One day you'll find someone. Sandy will too, whether it's you, or someone else. Raising kids takes all the help available. You need to snap out of it, get involved."

"Alfie marked May 31st on the calendar with a big black X."

"Good."

All the pages before the X used to give me comfort. Now there's just two months left, a thin paper wall slowly vanishing. "It's like that movie about a man who knows he'll have to go to prison on a certain day—"

"This is a baby we're talking about, not a prison sentence."

"I didn't say it was a prison sentence."

"If you're going to be a good father, you need to get up off your duff."

"I'm 24 years' old."

"I had your sister at 22." She glanced at me quickly. "I don't think I ever told you this, but I was pregnant when we got engaged. And then I miscarried, but we got married anyway and I got pregnant again. The first time I got pregnant, it was like the baby was stealing our youth. Going to be parents at 21. And then when I miscarried, it was like we were robbed, and so I got pregnant again." She put a hand on my thigh. "One day you'll look back on this in a completely different light."

This is how a 30 calibre bullet kills. Travelling at 2440 feet per second, the energy of the bullet pushes on skin and flesh which stretches until it ruptures enough to allow passage of the bullet. The tissue dissipates the energy of the bullet by fragmenting and tearing. While the flesh contracts back to near its original position, the bullet continues to travel through muscle, bone and organs, destroying nearly everything in its path.

Next morning, I was out before the sun was up. And this time I spotted them lumbering beside the fence: a pair of raccoons the size of small dogs. I raised the rifle. My thumb lowered the safety and my finger slipped inside the trigger guard as the sights came in line. I took a bead on the nearest animal, the larger one, and squeezed the trigger. The rifle sounded, kicked against my shoulder and threw me off balance. The nearest raccoon flopped onto its side, rolled a little. The other dashed under the fence into the shrubs, a waddle sped up so it seemed to lurch from side to side. I slid up the bolt, ejected the spent casing and fired again, but the animal was gone. Walking down the fence line, I fired into the shrub again and again while a liquid excitement pumped through my body. The rifle smashed into my shoulder until my arm was numb. Five shots and the clip was empty. My heart began to slow and I stepped over the dead raccoon where steam was already rising from a growing pool of blood.

Behind me the cottage door opened and closed. "My God," my mother shouted. "You killed them?" She was still tying a

93

bathrobe around herself.

"Just one."

"You were supposed to trap them not shoot them."

"Mom, this raccoon almost killed your cat."

"That's the mother. You killed the mother."

"How do you know which is the mother?"

She shook her head. "Oh Ryan, I just. Oh God."

"What is it?"

"I don't know. It's sad. They've been my company all this time."

I tucked the rifle's stock under my arm. "I honestly don't even understand why you're living up here with raccoons for company. Raccoons you ask me to get rid of then start crying over."

"I just wanted you to come up." She looked away, raised her shoulders and shivered. "I wanted to give you a chance to tell your news. It was all I could think of."

"Well, I didn't know. You should have said something."

A woman is considered to be in labour when she begins experiencing strong and regular uterine contractions accompanied by dilation of her cervix. Labour's first stage continues until the cervix is dilated to ten centimetres. The length of the second stage varies from twenty minutes to two hours. During this time, the mother pushes the baby from the womb with contractions spaced three to five minutes apart. This stage ends with the delivery of the baby.

After packing up that afternoon, I kicked the raccoon into a garbage bag. Its body had already stiffened in the cold. I dropped it in the trunk beside the rifle and my overnight bag.

"It's funny to think raccoon skins used to be worth something," Mom said. "The fur."

"Everything used to be worth something."

"Now we just pack it in a garbage bag and drive it to the

dump."

"You could skin it, make yourself a hat. Make one for the baby."

"It's just sad how we don't seem to care anymore. No-one cares about doing anything. I can't even knit a sweater for my grandchild."

"You've got plenty of time. It's spring. It's going to be summer."

Nodding, Mom stepped closer, put her arms around me. "Give this grandmother-to-be a big hug, okay. And one for you, wonderful father-to-be." She held me longer than she had in years. I'm not sure which of us broke away, but when we did, she was crying. She wiped each eye. "Oh this is silly."

"I'm going to talk to Sandy about maybe being around for the birth. Or maybe seeing the baby straight afterwards. Guess I should talk to her anyway."

My mother nodded. "Good. That's great. I'm proud of you."

I slid behind the wheel, rolled down my window and waved and honked as I pulled out of her lane. Once on the road, I put on a Moby CD and settled in for the drive.

A stillbirth occurs when a foetus, which has died in the womb or during labour exits the mother's body. Still relatively common in Canada, there are 7.7 stillbirths per thousand. The reasons for most human stillbirths are unknown, but causes include placental abruption, physical trauma, bacterial infection and chromosomal aberrations.

I got the news the moment I stepped into the apartment. Alfie had already listened to the message and he played it for me. It was Sandy's voice, thin and drawn. "I lost the baby." Her breath echoed through the phone. "And thought you should know."

Alfie had a bong hit lined up on the table. I sat by it,

fingered the lighter while from a great distance, from thousands of miles away, he said, "Dude, you dodged a bad one there."

I tossed the lighter onto the table and leaned back. "I don't know."

One of the tiny outfits Mom had bought was sticking out of the shopping bag, little feet built into the body, snaps all the way down the back. On the front, it said, "Sweet dreams till morning."

While Alfie reached for the bong, I pulled out that sleeper. From either side of the sofa, and from a long distance apart, we gazed at it.

ALICE PETERSEN

Among the Trees

What remained of Hugh had been delivered to Jan in a corrugated cardboard box, marked Temporary Container. Jan knew that Hugh would have been delighted, he would have positively roared with laughter at the aptness of the label, given that he had made it his life's work to celebrate the passing of time. She held the box with both hands while she made her way uphill through the bare forest, her coat snagging on the branches of fallen spruce. Eventually she arrived at a high rock where the cliff fell away toward the lake in a jumble of boulders and moss and clinging cedars. Across the lake, banks of cloud lay along the hills, and the birches stood arrayed in white stripes against the cocoa brown and blue of the land. It was as good a place as any to do the scattering.

She opened the box for the first time and looked doubtfully at the granular presence in the plastic bag. It was not Hugh in that box. Hugh would never have had anything to do with a plastic bag, or a twist-tie. Hugh was already out mingling with the other molecules in the air. He had always been everywhere and nowhere in particular.

Time to scatter, and she saw herself walking behind a plough, flinging seed in wide arcs. She could hear his gravelly voice, "It may be the most useful work of art I ever create. Ashes are good for plants." "Here darling," she said to him internally, "try arranging this." She flung the ashes out of the bag and they fell over the cliff edge not in a poetic swirl, but in a pattering shower like a fall of drops from a tree long after the rain has passed.

Jan had been 22 when she inherited the log cabin on the edge of the great forest of the Mauricie. Her grandparents, tweedy Anglican folk with quiet voices and expensive shoes, had recognized that Jan alone of all the Toronto clan would not immediately sell the Quebec fishing camp in exchange for a manicured rock in Georgian Bay. There had been no animosity in the family when the bequest was revealed. As Hugh put it, Jan's family was territorially gifted, and there were enough properties of one kind or another to keep all the descendants happy.

Built by wealthy Americans in the late nineteenth century, the pine-lined cabin had acquired a rich patina through repeated application of wood smoke and evening tobacco. Jan had studied albums of minute snapshots of men and women in knickerbockers posing with their catches, while local guides crouched in the background, their eyes hidden in the smoke from campfires, sleeves rolled up to expose their hard sun-darkened forearms. Jan had an interest in photography and an interest in history, and now she had inherited enough money to indulge in both.

About this time, Hugh found Jan in the way a very young woman sometimes dreams of being found and trapped under the hot spotlight of a powerful regard. The art gallery had been full, the people arranged in clusters in front of the paintings, gesturing with their wine glasses, some ignoring the paintings altogether and living only for the subtle readjustment in the room as each new person entered it. Jan was wearing the ruby silk that she had cut on the grain and the fabric swirled over her thighs. She feigned indifference to the stocky figure with his shorn white hair bristling like filaments, but at any time during the evening she could have told you exactly where "Hugh-the-sculptor" was to be found. A day later a chance meeting at the liquor store and two bottles of Chilean red wine resulted in hours and whole days in bed and out of it, as their two bodies locked together and tumbled again and again off a high cliff into the warm air.

Jan's life could not be the same afterwards. Hugh made the idea of answering the telephone in an art gallery seem like ridiculous work. Jan resigned from the job and began to take her photography seriously. She took Hugh off to spend the summer in the cabin in the woods.

At the beginning, a great crowd of friends visited the cabin. Seated in a protective ring of citronella candles, they ate berry compote off leaves and argued late into the night. When the mosquitoes became unbearable, they stripped and swam out along the drunken path of the moon. They were a mixed bunch, all happy to escape the Toronto heat. Vernon Hasp, the film maker, and his girlfriend Tiny made the long drive across to Quebec in a convertible. Tiny brought with her bowls of the whipped tofu and lemon delight that she manufactured in great quantities and which, as Hugh said, transmuted the contents of one's stomach to liquid gold. Zach Singer, the oboe player, came and he played while ageless Frederique Cyr danced, the humid air making a puddle of the mascara beneath her eyes. After supper Gypsa McNider recited poetry in the clearing under the birches, her batwing sleeves arcing through the air as she declaimed that the amount of love in the world was constant. Her partner Tim lounged in the shadows rolling joints.

Hugh always sat well back in his chair, legs splayed, hands clasped over his stomach, arguing and drinking and drinking some more. He was a sculptor, and nature was his medium, for Hugh's art celebrated the transience of the day. He spoke of creating with the fundamental drive of a bee or a robin, but it was his personal mission to make manifest the passage of time. A spy out before dawn might glimpse Hugh crouched close to the earth, aligning the cedar fronds on the path to the dock, so that they all pointed like arrows at a newly sprung toadstool capped in neon tangerine. Days later, the same fronds would be discovered placed in concentric circles honouring the fall of the same toadstool, its head now pock-marked and saggy with spores. Hugh alone knew how to rearrange a cobweb with a needle, scratch fern fronds onto a clear sheet of ice. The sight of Hugh lying face down on the dock, herding the skipping silver slips of the water beetles into a corral made of reeds threaded together on a horse hair filled Jan with the desire to shout out loud at the magnificence of life. His mode of being challenged Jan's conservative roots and it attracted her, held her, and she would not, could not stop giving him her love, for his art, for his vision, for his great arms and fists and for the gold cap on his tooth.

"Stay," she said to him. "Stay always. My forest is your forest, my woods are your woods, my leaves your leaves, my lake your lake, my streams your streams." She could remember the silly loving burble of words even now.

Once Hugh made Jan a stained-glass window, pieced together out of slips of mica leaded with reeds, glued with pine sap, girded with willow. The window was an impossible gift, and theirs was an impossible relationship, and yet it had lasted. For twenty years the summer colony in the woods had been a place of refuge for artists of all kinds. Hugh did not know, but after a gust of wind shattered the mica window, Jan had searched the forest floor for shards. She kept them in an envelope under a floorboard in the bedroom.

In the beginning Jan had considered Hugh's renunciation of permanence to be a grand and free gesture, like the operatic trilling of the hermit thrush or a soprano practising in a neighbouring house. She had honoured his anger when he had discovered her photographing his work. Hugh had knocked the camera out of her hand into the ferns, where she later picked it up, unharmed. Get out, he'd said. Get out of her own place. Extraordinary to think of it now, like that. And afterward he knelt before her and soaked her wraparound skirt with his tears.

"Your spirit is wide, Jan, like the horizon," he said, stretching out his arms to receive her. So she forgave him, and with him she felt forgiven.

Sometimes Jan finds it unbearable that Hugh should have seen her ageing. She ought to have drifted in and out of his life like one of his time-limited sculptures, here at dawn, gone in the evening, with the last trilling of the hermit thrush. Now she saw herself standing in the forest with an empty cardboard box in her thin cold hands, a withered woman in an olive coloured skirt and long boots. Botox and lifts she has rejected, her hair is shorter now, and she keeps it dark by artificial means, but she knows it disappoints people to come across her from behind, to have her turn to face them with the ridged pools of sleeplessness beneath her eyes.

Just as once upon a time Hugh found Jan, so he eventually found Crispin, one summer night in a bar on the Main in Montreal. Crispin was quick, wiry and witty. In another century he might have been a velvet-clad poet relishing his dreams, but Crispin was a water-colourist, producing exquisite works of the old school. They sold well. Dreamy clouds are never easy to achieve, but Crispin had a knack for painting the wide sky of Quebec on fire in the evening or nacreous at first light. Crispin's skies caught at the emotions, hinted at spiritual depth, but remained guileless, because when it came down to it, they were just sky, just water-colour.

Jan still has a photograph of Crispin at that time, lithe Crispin wearing a black halterneck with diamantes that stretch in a glittering curve into the hollows of his armpits. Earlier in the day they had pulled up the chains and anchors on the dock and had paddled off on it as if it were a raft. Crispin swam around in the water, his wet head coppery in the sunlight. He was playful as an otter. For a while they had all wanted him.

Jan had tried hard. She maintained outward appearances with meals and money, but somewhere she lost the knack of renewing her love for Hugh each day and she found herself acting more as she felt she ought to, rather than from desire. The parties in the woods changed. Vernon Hasp's documentary about other men called Vernon Hasp attained cult status and he began to hold court in his own penthouse where he could see himself reflected in sixteen panes of glass at a time. Tiny drifted off to farm organic carrots. Frederique died from complications following a hip replacement. Their places were taken by Crispin's friends, students, actors, musicians shouting at each other about Derrida and hip hop. Hugh was often absent from Jan's bed in the morning, but the woods revealed little trace of his work.

Jan knew better than to say anything. Hugh had every right to live as he wished. Early on she did her crying in a city bus, during one of those winters when she taught photography at a community college. The tears erupted when she least expected it, pouring out with all the shame and inevitability of vomit onto the sidewalk, while the high-school kids sitting around her sank into their jackets and looked out the window.

The next summer when they returned to the woods, Jan slept in the cabin and Hugh shuttled between her room and Crispin's in the Bunkie. One morning when she was out taking photographs she came across Crispin perched on a rock, brooding in the steam that rose off the lake into the cool morning.

"I do love him, you know," he said.

"You know nothing of love," she replied. That morning she took a photograph of a reed bending backwards into its sharply angled reflection. Around it quivered the lines of the water. The illusion of flexibility recalled her desire to share her streams and woods with Hugh, but when she looked at the bent reed she also remembered how hard it was to share Hugh.

Later in the day she woke Hugh from a nap, sat on the edge of the bed, spread out her hands on her knees, placed her ultimatum before him.

"I'm not cooking anymore," she said.

"I never said you had to."

"I don't want you sleeping in the cabin any more."

"I'll leave if you want me to, Jan."

"No, you must stay, but stay in the Bunkie. I'm not leaving you." It was all she had left to say. She could forgive Hugh for Crispin. Perhaps Hugh had discovered some great and good love in himself with Crispin that he had never experienced with Jan. She even told herself that she could stop desiring Hugh, if that was what he wanted, but she could not stop caring.

They did not see a couple's therapist, but they did see an architect; the architect of our separation, she called the rotund little man in his office tower of reflecting glass. They renamed the main cabin the "Ruche" or hive, and constructed a network of simple buildings, half hidden in the bedrock or up on stilts, with shutters that hid the windows, and ferns that grew upon the roof. Fireplaces and rock ledges jutted out into the sitting-rooms, and the buildings were joined by walkways with holes cut in them to accommodate the growth of the trees.

Jan built herself a studio on stilts where she worked on her photographs with an intensity that surprised her. Her subjects were clouds, trees, reflections. She made photo essays of the barns and shrines in the rural community around the lake, but she rarely took pictures of people. The only face for her remained Hugh's. He had a half smile of such infinite sweetness, made the sweeter by his capacity to withhold the same smile. She marked every day of their separation with a photograph: ice in the reeds, the minute coal bright sparks of the lichen flowers, the water droplets that filled the lichen goblets to the brim.

And so the years had passed. During the summers they lived in a scattered way under the trees, with Crispin, without Crispin, with Crispin again. And little by little Hugh's skin took on the transparency of age and little by little Jan's photographs became all the same. Up on the cliff top, with the empty container in her hand, Jan saw how she had lorded it over Hugh in her ownership of the paradise, and somewhere she had lost the natural line of herself, the line that swirled, was elastic and cut on the grain. Glorying in the idea of doing what she said she would do, she had given Hugh a place to stay, always, and in her stubbornness she had made chains for them both.

But she had done what she said she would do. She had shared. By God she shared everything that she had, and now when she finally had it all to herself, the wind lifting the roof in the old cabin, the rattle of fly abdomen against the glass in the studio, she found that she did not want it.

Perhaps Hugh had been right in his insistence that there should be nothing left to mark his passage in the world, no child, no artwork, no monument, nothing. Let the cabin and the studio on stilts fall into a careless teepee of boards in the forest, and beneath it a stained kapok mattress, its sodden insides spilling out into the leaf mould. Maybe there is no virtue, after all, in doing what you said you were going to do. Gone were the days of Frederique lifting her chiffon scarves to the poplars. Jan shrugged. Now Hugh was gone too, and what was the point of holding on to anything? The time had come to pull her resentment out of herself, this anchor of hatred and love, and the gobbet of flesh that it was attached to. Up came the cable, dripping and straining, encrusted with zebra mussels and streaming weed. Mentally she flung it off the cliff after the ashes, left it to coil like a dead snake caught in a cedar tree.

Jan turned away from the cliff's edge and started back down the track. Out of habit she caught herself observing the funnelled spiderwebs and the woodpecker holes, the flaps of lichen attached to the rock faces. It was 20 November, 2003 and Hugh had begun his passage into the ground, but she had no camera, no way to mark this day. Tomorrow the day would be gone. And now the tears came, for there was no other pair of eyes to see, to verify or to contradict her version of the vision. He was a bastard to have left her so alone.

Jan reached the bottom of the hill. In the distance she could see the huddle of men beside the cars strung out along the road. Crispin was in the middle of the group, no longer young, but preserved by the passage of good scotch and regular exercise. Four young friends stood about, their beards groomed into neat pubic triangles. Hugh had been in thrall, more so than ever toward the end, trapped by loneliness and the camaraderie of rough young sex in treehouses.

The men looked at the cold sky and at the cold land, their hands thrust deep into their jacket pockets. Then they turned to look at her, expectant.

"Well, he's out there," she said, showing them the empty container. She waited for Crispin to speak. Now it was time to see what Crispin would make of the scattered remains of Hugh's love.

"God, I'm so very sorry," said Crispin, breathing in deeply and covering his face.

She stood looking at the backs of Crispin's hands, reddened and dry with cold, sparkling with short golden hairs. What was Crispin to her now? He was certainly not a son, or a brother, but some other relation—a step-partner, from whom she expected nothing, and to whom she owed nothing. And yet, she thought, it was true, she had also passed a life of sorts with Crispin.

Hugh was gone, but nothing was finished. Together they had built a colony, and the history of a colony is filled with coming, and going, and coming back again. The words came out of Jan before she could stop them.

"Stay," she said to Crispin. "Stay. Invite your friends. There's plenty of vegetable soup in the pot." Her mouth stretched sideways in an elastic line, and there was a give in it that she had forgotten.

Crispin took his hands away from his face and reached out to touch her forearm. His eyes were paler than ever now that he taken to bleaching his hair.

"Thanks for the offer Jan," he said, "you've been a sweetie. But I think we'll head back into town. Mike has a gig tonight. Don't you Mike?"

A young man in black leather nodded, jingling his car keys.

"Right," said Jan. "Well. Come up whenever you feel like it." She turned away, holding herself rigid against the cold. Crispin stopped her as she was unlocking the car.

"Jan," he said, "Hugh stayed because he wanted to. Don't doubt that."

Jan spent the night at the cabin. She did not light the fire and she did not heat the soup. Instead she cocooned in the duvet and lay listening to the scuffle and twitter of mice in the walls. In the night the first snows came, and when she awoke she looked out at the fir trees and their green fingers, now outlined in white, spread wide and ready to bless. So that was it, she thought, the final benediction. She was 44, and free to go.

After Summer

Jake and I grew up without a mother, which was not that bad, although we ate a lot of boiled peas. Back when we were kids, before Maybelle came into the picture, Dad used to rent a boathouse for the whole of August up on a lake near Shawinigan. He spent the summer months growing a fat Hemingway moustache while the sun darkened his shoulders to the colour of beer. We weren't supposed to sleep at the boathouse, but in early August when the concrete city had baked hard in the sun, Dad would drive us up to the lake on Friday night. We'd light citronella candles to keep the mosquitoes off, eat rubbery pizza and drink warm juice out of the cooler. After the bats came out, we'd go up into the woods to pee before going to sleep in a row on the boathouse floor, listening to the water lapping and Dad breathing in the dark.

On Saturday mornings Dad sat in the boathouse attic typing up the poems that he carried in his head during the rest of the year. The poems were mainly about women, glimpsed through panes of frosted glass, since Dad was a mail carrier with two kids and that's about as close as he ever got. If you stood at the bottom of the ladder you could hear Dad up there snorting out lines about galoshes and garden paths, white terriers and white negligees, the day-long ning-nong of the bell and endless waiting for a snug fit in scented flesh.

While Dad worked at his poems Jake and I squatted on the dock making fat duck farting noises by blowing through blades of grass. Sometimes we would stir the water with sticks, or catch horseflies and hand deliver them into the webs of the dock spiders. Dad was in his confessional, and we were being mostly good. Eventually Dad would climb back down the ladder, his skin smelling of hot pine boards and the edgy stench of the bats that lived behind the rafters, and then we would all swing off the rope on the tree and drop into the water.

I have this vision of Dad at the lake during the long summers, emerging from the waves, his chest hair gathered in dripping points. Shaggy Dad, Poseidon Dad, ever-strong Dad, and Jake and me screaming and clinging onto him like monkeys, while he dunked us up and down. And eventually he would say "Clear off, I feel a poem coming on," and he would grab a couple of beers out of the cooler dug into the shallows and disappear up the ladder into the attic room to write, while we sidled off to the cliffs to look for fossils.

Once we didn't clear off, instead we dragged a ladder out of the grass and propped it up against the boathouse wall. Jake was just peering in at the window at the top when a rotten rung of the ladder gave way and he fell and knocked himself out.

"Dad's got no clothes on and he's crying," he said when he woke up, by which time Dad was fully dressed and driving into town as fast as he could.

It hadn't occurred to us that Dad might be unhappy, because we weren't, and it was summertime, and Dad was just Dad. We knew he drank each night on the boathouse steps, but it did not bother us. The more beer he drank the more bottles there were to get a refund on.

Just after we turned fourteen, Dad started dating Maybelle, and that was the end of summers at the lake, because there was no plug at the boathouse for her hairdryer.

Maybelle was a secretary at our high school. She took it on to rescue Dad from the two giant squid choking him in their tentacled embrace. First she moved in and began cooking balanced meals, which in itself was not a bad thing, but then she persuaded Dad to give up mail delivery and open a dry-cleaning business. There was an office out the back where Maybelle talked on the phone to tardy clients, threatening to send their suits and dresses to Colombia in a container ship if they did not come to collect them. "Most companies don't bother to phone," she would say. My father pressed the trousers. The heat made his hair damp and curled behind his ears. I worked the cash after school. I liked the punking noise the receipts made when you stuck them on the spike. Jake refused to have anything to do with it.

A couple of years after Dad hooked up with Maybelle, Jake slipped the net and hitchhiked to Big Sur. Four years passed and Maybelle spotted him on a home renovating show, making a plywood stereo cabinet on a suburban front lawn, satisfying women across North America with the kerthunk of his nail gun and the hiss and judder of the compressor. He was giving the camera his long lazy grin and he had his ball cap at a howdy pardner tilt. The dentist always said that Jake had too many teeth, but he had enough for television.

After Jake lit out I stayed on, typing out my angst one finger at a time on Dad's Olivetti in badly spaced, incredibly awful, rhyming verse about hideous misunderstandings and imagined perfect communion. After I had written each poem, I would shred it and let my geriatric gerbils make a nest of my thoughts. I was slightly chubby, hopelessly normal.

I haven't spent my life looking for a mother, and I certainly haven't looked for one in Maybelle. Maybelle keeps her hair pretty. Maybelle sews sofa cushions. She is a wreath of dried-flowers-with-seasonal-bear-on-the-front-door kind of person. I haven't missed out on mothering, but I'm kind of missing Dad. Maybelle has Dad cornered like a bull, down on his Hemingway knees, helpless beneath the weight of house and car payments. He's slapped daily by the coats on the electric rack at the dry cleaner's as they flare out and twirl around the corner. But he seems happy. I have to be honest about that. Maybe Dad has a good time between her satin sheets.

The other weekend I drove out to buy a chair just like the one Dad used to sit on to write his poetry. Dad's chair had a woven seat made of some kind of hide, thick and yellow like old cooked pasta, which we always thought of as cat gut, since Dad emitted such excruciating yowls during his bouts of work. The chair had no screws in it, just wooden plugs and when Dad stretched back the chair creaked from the hip joint. Not a comfortable chair, but a speaking chair that moaned along with Dad's efforts to express himself. Of course we had to leave it behind in the boathouse with all the other stuff that was never ours.

I drove out across the plain toward St. Eulalie, thinking of the time when it had been boreal forest, and how the rustling leaves must have roared in the wind, like the sea in the fall. My dog had her head out the passenger window. Flecks of saliva whipped off her tongue and attached themselves to the rear door. There never was a dog with so much saliva, or such perpetual anticipation of the good to come.

At the antique store, a dog with a golden plume of a tail rushed out to sniff at my dog and at my shoes. The store was a real barn of a place hung with mooseheads and ancient egg-beaters, and leather pouches of oxidizing fishing hooks. Most of the furniture had been scraped and repainted, as if the years had not given it enough story, so story had to be added to it.

I asked about chairs, and was directed upstairs to a stifling room under the rafters, filled with golden light that came through panels let into the ceiling. At one end were stacks of tables: end tables, side tables with barley twist legs, dining-room tables, bedside tables with drawers, washstands; so many surfaces for putting down cups, saucers, books, type-writers and beer bottles. And of course there were also hundreds of chairs spooning into each other, battered, scraped, loose bottomed, straw filled, hide bound chairs, which meant that there were hundreds of lapsed poets, hundreds of adult children looking for lost fathers, and hundreds of family stories about stepmothers, which when it came down to it, were not so different one from another. The weight of all those chairs hanging in the rafters filled me with airless panic.

After Maybelle came there was none of the tangy essence of bat left about my father. The moist air of drycleaning softened Dad's poems and turned them to powdery mould. And now Dad's going to marry Maybelle and after I've signed him over as a going concern, I wonder when I'll be talking to him again, because it's his life now, and he's chosen to live like that, with her and her dried flowers. I just wish that Jake would slouch on in with his arms crossed over his chest and smile in his lazy summer dog way, because I really want to take him out for a beer and ask him if he thinks that we somehow made Dad feel smothered when we clung on to him. I mean, when he dunked us in the water, did he ever wish that he had let us go? And now that we are twenty, has he at last let us go? And if he has, what is it like to tread water alone, without even a chair to hold onto when the spring floods come?

Salsa Madre

Come on in, don't be shy. My name is Bernadette. And you are? Jan. So pleased to meet you, Jan. Father René told me that you would stop by. Yes, I always work out here under the carport. I like the sound of rain falling on the roof. You're from Montreal? Toronto. Ah. That's a long way. I have a niece who lives there, on Yonge Street. Twins in a stroller, maybe you have seen her? They're a handful of trouble. Well, this is my summer project—should be finished in the next day or two. Sure, photos are fine. You might find the ground more stable for your tripod over on the path.

These are my tiles and pots and cups, arranged by colour. I do the actual smashing on the concrete, and I shape the pieces afterwards with nippers. I use an outdoors glue to fix the ceramic to the bathtub. Here's a nice piece of Limoges that Madame Benoit passed on to me. Look at the pink dress on that courtly lady, but see how it's cracked underneath? There's gold paint on it. I'll be using it somewhere special.

Today I prayed that the paint inside my shrine would stay put. I will not be ashamed to ask for that in the church, since my work is to glorify the Mother of Our Lord, so the paint should not flake no matter what I do. Not to say you shouldn't prime carefully. After all, our God is a busy God. I've seen shrines where the sun gets in and the paint hangs down in sheets around the head of the Holy Mother. She stands there as if she'd got her head up under a string of washing. Shame.

Mind you, not many people bother to keep up their shrines any more, and I don't know that you're going to find anything other than empty ones around here. These days people prefer deer on their lawns, or roosters or kids fishing. Down on Rue Bonaventure someone has a Montreal Stadium being attacked by a giant polar bear. Not many people feel that much faith any more, or if they do, they keep it up their sleeves and not in their gardens, except at Christmas, and then it's the plastic statues. Violette La Caisse bought an entire set on sale at the hardware store and they faded after two years. You can't make holy things out of plastic.

I've been doing mosaic stars on my bathtub, rays or petals of one colour and centres of another. I stick them on first, and then I fill in the gaps after with little bits left over. Mother Mary approves of recycling. She gave birth in a barn, after all, even though where she is now she probably has most things in gold and jasper. I gave her statue a clean this morning. She looks nice lying on the grass, doesn't She? Resting. Just like my mother used to have a lie-down after lunch.

I expect Father René told you that I was once a novice. I was about to take my vows when God came to me in a dream. He said go to the general store, so I did. I was so shy! The store was nothing like the supermarkets we have now. You could get anything there. Violette La Caisse was working the till that day. Urgel Beauregard from up Lac des Tortues way came in. I didn't know him from Adam, but I heard him say to Violette that his wife had died and would she have him, because he had six children and didn't know what he would do. And Violette said thanks for offering, but she had enough on her hands with the rush on sugar pie orders, and she turned to serve me and I looked up at Urgel's big empty eyes. He drove a truck for the paper mill, and I brought up all those children in this house and we had two more of our own. Good kids. They all pitched in.

Now I'm going to tell you what happened to my son Henri. It's nothing you won't hear from down the road. Still, I'd rather tell you in my own words. People say that divorce is the worst thing that can happen to a family, but there are worse things. It's the same with families as it is with ceramic. You don't know quite how the tile will crack, even if you think you have a rough idea. I'm talking hairline cracks, places where it's ready to break and we can't tell until the hammer comes down. Well, whatever went on used to happen in the vestry. And in the end my boy Henri got so quiet I knew something was up. He was not the only one. And next thing they sent that priest to the South of France so that he could do it all over again in the sun.

When Henri turned sixteen he went to work in his uncle's fish shop in Montreal. Plenty of boys do it. I suppose they think there's more to life down there. Hard to imagine, isn't it? When we have all this sky up here. But at least he told me he was going—he could have gone to do squeegee like that kid down the road. I left him alone. You have to let people work things out, but I never stopped wondering how he was, and I never stopped praying for him. He was a good kid.

You know, about this time last year, the Virgin Mary appeared to me behind the barn. I was spraying the lettuces with a slug killer that I make by boiling up cigarette butts. It works a charm. Well all of a sudden I had this feeling that there was a mystery happening beyond the edge of the vegetable patch. And I came around the corner of the barn, and there She was, hovering over the lightning weed. Just small, like a statue, but shimmering. And she said to me in a voice as low as a mourning dove's, *Find what was lost, renew what has been broken, give the thanks that is due.* I fell down to my knees and I cried and I cried.

Well, what can you do when the Holy Mother calls? I went to Montreal on the bus and stayed with my cousin's friend Rosalia. She lives near the Jean Talon market. So beautiful this market, with the fruit laid out in the shops—pink carrots, pink! You've got organic bananas spooning to the left, aubergines spooning to the right, and prickly fruits from Asian countries that I don't even know the name of. I bought a lot of tomatoes for only five dollars, and Rosalia and I spent all afternoon making a sauce called salsa madre, which is very good and has more garlic in it than Urgel would ever let me use at home. I had no trouble discovering where Henri was living. He has an apartment in the Church of Our Lady of the Immaculate Conception, only now it's condos. Early in the morning I sat in the band rotunda in the park, and I saw them come out of the door, my Henri, and a little boy, and another man.

The boy sat on Henri's shoulders and held onto his ears for balance. Henri's friend held the door open for them, shut it carefully behind them. I can tell you, I was alight with joy in my veins. The urge to get up and run to them, God help me, it was so strong. But I screwed my feet to the floor. I watched them walk all the way down the street to the car, a nice car. Then I went back to Rosalia's and got the jars of salsa madre, and then I returned to the church that is now condos. A young man with a ponytail let me into the building. He had a T-shirt on that said "Don't shut me in." I looked at him and said with my eyes, "Don't shut me out," and he opened the door, just like that.

Inside, you have no idea what they have done to the Church of Our Lady. They have built a hotel in there, and left one pew to sit on while you wait for the elevator. Where there should be a stoup, just inside the door, there is a water cooler. And where the Cardinal walked on marble flagstones in 1961, there is carpet and a corridor. Well I've done the same thing in the other direction, me out here turning my bathtub into a sacred place. We're all going in one direction or another, and who's to say it won't become a church again in a hundred years? Likewise, if you needed a bathtub, you could come and dig up one of those empty shrines from down the road.

From Henri's apartment on the fifth floor you can see the whole city. A young woman was there, doing the cleaning. Such a tiny wee thing from some Asian country. She could see I was his mother, and she showed me right in. Oh, such an apartment you have never seen! So tidy, so calm, like a

116

monastery, with slanted windows high in the ceiling, and a shining aluminum refrigerator, and a bedroom up a spiral staircase. Like apartments in New York, I am sure. I delivered my jars of salsa madre, and the girl stood on a chair and put them in an empty cupboard high up, and we lined up the jars just so and closed the doors. Henri will find them on a hungry day, a day when he cannot think what to cook, and he can use that sauce with the vegetables that he might already have. So that was it. I came home. I don't like Montreal. Too much concrete. But at least I know that he is living in the house and heart of Our Lady, and he is safe. And I am glad, and grateful for Prayers Answered. And so I wait, in case Henri wants to bring that child home to meet his grandmother, because that is the next thing that I will pray for, as I pray for the man who held the door open, and the mother of the child, too, whoever she is. I will wait and watch for Henri to come in his own time, same as I wait for the deer to come out of the forest to eat the new shoots on the field. And then, what a feast we will have.

Look, Jan—I am ready for the coulis. How do you call coulis in English? Yes, grout. The colour of this grout is called paprika, which will spice up all that blue and make the yellow bright even in the rain. So we mix up the coulis with water, until it's thick and sloppy like icing, and then we work it on with a spatula, like this, into the cracks, and then scraping off the excess, and then doing it again. Here we go. And now we give a good polish with our cloth, et voilà, the colours come together and my bath becomes a shrine fit for Our Lady of Lowing Cows, Our Lady of Meltwater, Our Lady of Lightning Weed, Our Lady of Blackened Shingles, Our Lady of the Smelter, Our Lady of Everywhere.

Without the coulis, the broken cups and saucers are just that, broken. And without the ceramic, the coulis is just wet earth. But put both together, and they glow. The coulis is love. We cannot do without it. You have kids, Jan? Just your books of photographs? Well, it's all for the glory. Will you listen to that blackbird? He's up there every evening. Let me wash my hands and I'll fix you some coffee. You won't find a better cup down the road.

REBECCA ROSENBLUM has just completed a master's degree in English and creative writing at the University of Toronto. Her work has been published in *The Danforth Review, Exile, echolocation, The New Quarterly, Qwerty, Ars Medica* and *The Journey Prize Stories 19*. Her first collection of short stories, *Once*, received the Metcalf-Rooke Award for Fiction and will be published in the fall of 2008.

DANIEL GRIFFIN has lived in Guatemala, New Zealand, England, Scotland, France and the US, but now lives in Victoria, BC with his wife and three daughters. His stories have appeared in numerous publications including *Grain, Prairie Fire, Geist, The New Quarterly* and *The Journey Prize Stories 16*. He is finishing his first book, *Mercedes Buyer's Guide*, a collection of stories about domestic life from the male perspective. See www.danielgriffin.ca.

ALICE PETERSEN grew up in New Zealand. Her short fiction has been published in *Takahe, Geist,* the anthology *Short Stuff: New English Writing in Quebec* and *The Journey Prize Stories 19*. In 2007, her stories were shortlisted for the Writers' Union of Canada Short Story Competition, the CBC Literary Awards and the Journey Prize. Petersen lives in Montreal, but she prefers to be up in the woods.

MARK ANTHONY JARMAN has published two collections of stories, *New Orleans Is Sinking* and *19 Knives*, and a travel book, *Ireland's Eye*. His hockey novel *Salvage King Ya!* is on Amazon.ca's list of 50 Essential Canadian Books, and he has won the Gold Medal at the National Magazine Awards. He is the fiction editor of *Fiddlehead* and teaches at UNB. A new collection of stories, *My White Planet*, will be published in 2008.

Previous volumes in this series contained stories by the following writers:

2007: Julie Paul, Fabrizio Napoleone, Anik See
2006: Roseanne Harvey, Larry Brown, Joel Katelnikoff
2005: Barbara Romanik, J.M. Villaverde, Jasmina Odor
2004: Neil Smith, Maureen Bilerman, Jaspreet Singh
2003: Liam Durcan, Andrea Rudy, Jessica Grant
2002: Chris Labonté, Lawrence Mathews, Kelly Cooper
2001: J.A. McCormack, Ramona Dearing, Goran Simic
2000: Christine Erwin, Vivette J. Kady, Timothy Taylor
1999: Marcus Youssef, Mary Swan, John Lavery
1998: Leona Theis, Gabriella Goliger, Darryl Whetter
1997: Elyse Gasco, Dennis Bock, Nadine McInnis
1996: Lewis DeSoto, Murray Logan, Kelley Aitken
1995: Warren Cariou, Marilyn Gear Pilling, François
      Bonneville
1994: Donald McNeill, Elise Levine, Lisa Moore
1993: Gayla Reid, Hannah Grant, Barbara Parkin
1992: Caroline Adderson, Marilyn Eisenstat, Marina
      Endicott
1991: Ellen McKeough, Robert Majzels, Patricia Seaman
1990: Peter Stockland, Sara McDonald, Steven Heighton
1989: Brian Burke, Michelle Heinemann, Jean Rysstad
1988: Christopher Fisher, Carol Anne Wien, Rick Hillis
1987: Charles Foran, Patricia Bradbury, Cynthia Holz
1986: Dayv James-French, Lesley Krueger, Rohinton
      Mistry
1985: Sheila Delany, Frances Itani, Judith Pond
1984: Diane Schoemperlen, Joan Fern Shaw, Michael
      Rawdon
1983: Sharon Butala, Bonnie Burnard, Sharon Sparling
1982: Barry Dempster, Don Dickinson, Dave Margoshes
1981: Peter Behrens, Linda Svendsen, Ernest Hekkanen
1980: Martin Avery, Isabel Huggan, Mike Mason

Most of these books are still available. Please inquire.